aHunter4Rescue

By

Cynthia A Clement

Print Edition
ISBN: 978-0-9920189-2-4

Book Cover designed by RomCon®
Cover photo - © CURAphotography - Fotolia.com

Dedication

To my husband and son, who supported my vision and put up with the clutter, late meals, and take-out until I finished.

Chapter 1

Ardal had followed orders without question for thirty-five years, but not this time. Bred to be a Hunter, he had always known death would be his reward. There was no fear in death, but there should be honor. He scanned the prison cage, taking a long look at each of his men. They were brothers and friends, and every one of them had been slotted for execution. Since time began, Hunters had existed, but now their breed was to be exterminated.

His men deserved better.

They deserved to die fighting.

He was the last of the clan Rioge; the last leader. His men were the only Hunters left. The rest of his race and brotherhood had been destroyed long before his unit had returned from their covert mission. Torture and violence had not elicited the information that the Holman wanted. He and his men would never break, so their usefulness was at an end. Now all that remained was death.

Every leader knew that the decision to risk lives must be weighed against the likelihood of winning. Their chances of winning were slim. The confines of the spacecraft and their chains almost guaranteed it. The time for a reprieve had come and gone. Their jailors were preparing the tubes that would shoot them into space to die a slow suffocating death. As resistors and convicted traitors, they were not deserving of a more humane execution.

There was only one decision.

They would fight and die as Hunters.

Ardal nodded at Garguin, who in turn passed the message down the line. Within seconds his unit of warriors and elite Hunters were ready for his signal. As the leader he would be the first to be executed. When they came for him he would make his move. The others would follow their training. The clang of the metal door opening sent icy resolve through his body.

The moment had come.

Ardal tightened his muscles and felt the familiar rush of adrenaline pulse through his body. He was a finely tuned weapon. Centuries of genetic modification and years of training had made him a formidable force. His jailors were no match for him. They were of the slave race, thinner boned and slow witted. The Holman had not seen the need for elite soldiers. They assumed a Hunter was incapable of disobeying an order. That would be Ardal's only advantage.

Three men came for him. He eased his breathing and slowed his heart rate before glancing once more at Garguin. He sent his orders. Only Hunters were capable of mind connection and it was a well-guarded secret of the brotherhood.

"When these are defeated, move the men from the cage. We fight until the last man is dead. We will die as soldiers."

"By Cygnus and Warrior your orders will be obeyed. It is an honor serving with you." Garguin turned away and nodded to the next in command.

Ardal moved his head from side to side, easing his muscles in preparation for battle. It was done. There was no turning back. They were now truly traitors. He focused on the men coming for him, complacent in their belief that they were in control.

Fools.

No man was safe from a Hunter.

Ardal assessed the man nearest him as a muscle bound oaf. The next was slightly built and walked with confidence. He had the look of one trained in hand to hand combat. The last was the leader and a coward judging by the distance he was careful to keep between him and the other jailors. He tightened his grip on the chains holding his hands together.

The oaf unlocked him from the cage.

"Not so tough now," his voice mocked before Ardal wrapped his chains around his neck and silenced him. The keys dropped from the jailor's hands. Ardal kicked them toward Garguin before rushing forward against the other men. He moved beyond the cage doors, leaving the way free for his men.

An elbow strike to the head of the second man kept him at bay until he had broken the neck of the oaf. Then he kicked free of the body and grappled with the next combatant. He fielded the man's hand chops, weaving and deflecting the blows with ease. He did not have time for finesse. He leveled a bone breaking kick to the man's ribs and then a knee to his head before using his chains to twist his neck and fling him at the last man.

A gun fired red heat in his direction, but the aim was deflected by the oncoming body. Ardal's eyes narrowed. He had been right. The man was a coward hiding behind his weapon. He pounced on the last jailor and forced the gun up against the man's chest just as he fired a second time. The man slumped against Ardal, his eyes startled as pain convulsed his body. It was a look Ardal was all too familiar with. Death.

Gauguin was at his side, unlocking the chains that still bound his hands together. "The crew will be alerted now."

"Divide the men and move through the craft." Ardal rubbed his wrists before bending to pick up the gun. "Kill all you see. No one is to be left alive. Arm yourself as you go."

Garguin nodded and motioned the men into separate groups before following Ardal. Their footsteps were silent, but the alarm had been signaled. Pounding footfall came toward them. Ardal moved into the shadows and braced for the fight.

They fought their way through men and bodies until they reached the control center of the craft. It was a modern ship, built for speed not battle. It was large enough to transport several thousand troops, or prisoners. They had encountered and defeated about six hundred men, a meagre amount for Ardal's unit of two hundred.

The heart of the craft was different. It was guarded by doors and locks, not men.

"Find explosives." Ardal ordered before turning back to the sealed encasement of the cockpit. "We need to gain control if there is any hope of survival."

His fingers moved over the grey metal of the massive security doors, exploring every niche and crevice of its cold steel. There were secrets to find here. Ardal followed a coated wire that lead from the door to the floor. He pulled on it with no effect. If there was a way to open the doors without force, he didn't find it.

Garguin returned and Ardal watched as Firbin, the youngest of his Hunters started applying the molding explosives to the doors. His fingers moved sure and confident, filling the cracks of the hinges and then across the opening seam. The boy might only be twenty-two, but he was a genius with explosives.

The blast ripped the doors apart with a force that shook the entire ship. Gunfire from inside the cockpit filled the air. Ardal kept his men away from the ragged opening until the shots stopped and then they went into the breach to fight. One by one the soldiers defending the cockpit fell until there was only the captain and his crew at the helm.

"Don't come any closer." The Captain pointed a laser pistol at the control panel. "I won't have my ship taken by traitors."

The Captain was shorter and slighter built than the other men at the helm. He had no facial hair, but his other features were similar to Hunters. His larger eyes, narrow nose, and small mouth marked him as an Ancient. He was of the ruling class on Cygnus, there before the Hunters and slave races. Some thought of them as Gods, but Ardal knew differently. The Captain's insignia proclaimed that he was a Holman.

Ardal tilted his head and glanced at the man's nametag. "I am impressed Captain Eamon. You are the first Holman I have met who is not a coward."

"You and your men are better dead. There is no place for you in the new regime." The Captain did not hide his disdain. "You were no better than slaves for the Kaladin, and where are they now?

"You would never have kept us alive this long unless you thought you could break us." Ardal took a step closer to the man. "You might hold us in contempt, but even torture and death will not force us to tell you where the last of the high council is hidden."

"It will do them no good." The Captain tightened his grip on his pistol. "The Holman have defeated the old ways. Now our people will have a chance to flourish."

"By conquering other planets?" Ardal watched Garguin and his men spread out in the control center. "That way only leads to destruction."

"You weren't bred to think." The Captain spat his scorn at Ardal. "You aren't even men in the truest sense of the word!"

Ardal moved in unison with his men. They killed the rest of the crew as he grabbed the Captain by the neck. He jerked him close, reaching for the pistol at the same time. He was too late to stop the reflex action of his captive. The gun fired at the bank of navigation computers. Exploding fragments and flames leapt everywhere. He threw the Captain away from him.

"Can you fix it Jehon?"

A tall broad-shouldered Hunter stepped forward with an extinguisher and sprayed the flaming bank of computers. Then he inspected the damage before shaking his head and stepping back.

"We are being pulled in by the gravity of that planet. We cannot avoid it."

Ardal nodded and looked through the floor-to-ceiling viewing window. A large planet loomed close, its globe shape filling most of the viewing screen. You did not have to be an expert in physics to know that the odds of survival were slim. He grabbed the Captain. There was only one thing left to do.

"Now you will see how real men die."

Ardal dragged Eamon out of the room. The rest of his men followed until they reached the padded area of the launching chamber. This was where passengers strapped themselves in for takeoff and landing of the spacecraft. It was built with heat shields and heavier metal to cocoon and protect its occupants from rough landings. He threw the Captain into one of the chairs and strapped him in.

"What is this planet that we are going to collide with?"

"M212.

"I have never heard of it." Ardal took a seat and nodded for his men to follow. Within seconds, everyone was secure.

"It's primitive, with numerous languages. Their technology is almost non-existent. Hell, they're still going to war against each other."

"Jehon, download a translator."

Ardal's training kicked in. He slowed his breathing and allowed his body to relax. All tension left his muscles as he prepared for a crash landing. Mentally he commanded his men to do the same.

The Captain's hands gripped his seat. "There's no chance we'll live. Use the emergency capsules. We'd have a better chance of surviving entry."

Ardal raised an eyebrow. "Frightened?"

"It's foolish to sit here and wait for the end." The Captain moved his hand to undo his straps, but Ardal stopped him.

"A Captain goes down with his ship." Ardal's voice was neutral, his judgement suspended. He was a Hunter, bred to obey orders and ensure that others followed. The Captain would do his duty.

Eamon's voice rose in a high pitched whine. "My men are dead, what difference does it make now?"

"Courage Captain. There is honor yet to be earned."

Jehon cleared his throat. "I've determined the most likely landing area and have the translator ready."

Ardal nodded. "Connect us. We may yet survive to fight another day. It has been a privilege leading you, Hunters true and right."

"By Cygnus and Warrior you have led us fine." The men's voices rose in unison.

Pride surged through Ardal. His men had not failed him. Even as they faced certain death, they remained calm. The ship's frame began to shake and the metal surrounding them glowed red. They were entering the atmosphere of the planet. They would probably perish in the air before a collision with the ground could kill them. Still, he could die in peace. He had given his men honor in their death. No greater duty did a leader have.

Chapter 2

The screeching roar of an explosion woke Fiona. The heavens were erupting into a million colors and dropping shards of flames around her. She had dozed off for a few minutes and now everything was burning bright. She glanced up. It was a crisp August night and the sky was bright and beautiful, perfect for viewing the Perseids.

That's why she'd come out to the center of her property to lie on the hood of her truck. She had watched the meteor shower until sleep had claimed her. It took a second to register that the stars were still in place. It was the ground around her that was consumed with fire and debris.

A plane crash!

Fiona jumped off her truck. The air smelled of burning fuel and the unmistakable odor of burnt flesh. It was a smell she'd hoped never to experience again, but here it was, all around her. The main crash was a distance away. If there were survivors, they'd need help.

There was no time to waste.

She grabbed the truck keys and took off over the field toward the red glow at the edge of the forest. If she'd lived in a city, thousands would have responded, but she was living in a remote part of Northern Canada and was probably the only one to see the crash.

The truck bounced and rocked from side to side as she drove over rocks and twigs. The complete darkness of the bush meant the only thing visible was the bright flames of the crash site. An opening in the trees gave her a full view of the damage. The truck's headlights illuminated the area.

It was a scene straight from hell.

Debris was scattered for acres. What had once been a field of small pine saplings, was now charred black. Flames leapt from sapling to sapling leaving black ash in their wake. Everywhere she looked was devastation. What had taken nature years to grow had been undone in seconds.

Fiona closed her eyes and fought back the tears. The property had been a haven of peace for her. Now all she would see was the burnt and scorched ground. Almost as if God wanted to give her a constant reminder of what her life had become. She groaned and forced herself to look at the scene. There was no changing it. Thank God the pond would stop the spread of the fire. The ground had frost on it and it had been a wet summer, so she doubted she'd have to call for fire suppression. She turned her head away from the burning trees and then back toward the crash.

Out of the flames came a man.

A survivor!

He was a giant of a man. He walked with a quick sure step. There was no hesitation or sign of injury in his pace. Strength, power, and command were evident in every stride he took as he moved closer to the truck. This was a man to be obeyed. Fiona shivered. She should have gone back to the house and called for help.

More men followed. People needed rescuing. The nearest town was at least thirty minutes away. She could help some, but the most serious would require a hospital. Even with four years of medical school and one year interning, she wasn't equipped to handle more than basic first aid.

She pulled the parking brake on the truck. The lead man was already at her vehicle and pulled the door open. Up close he was even more intimidating. Tall and broad shouldered, his hair and face were covered with soot and ash. He looked to be wearing a uniform, but half of his shirt was burned away. The other half did nothing to cover the ripples of muscles and raw strength of the man.

Fear clawed at Fiona's stomach.

"Yarda." His voice was hoarse and his face expressionless.

Her breath caught in her throat and her body began to shake. Physically, this man could crush her. She'd spent the last year in hiding and now her worse nightmare had fallen into her life. There would be no escaping. Fiona took a deep breath and stilled her fear. She couldn't assume every man meant to hurt her.

"Do you speak English?" Her voice was a low whisper.

"Versom." The giant glared at her.

Fiona put up her hand, ignoring the tremors. "I don't understand. What language are you speaking?"

The man pulled a small phone-like gadget from his pocket. He punched a few buttons and held it to her face. "Yarda."

"English." Fiona enunciated in a clear voice. "I don't understand your language.

The man looked down at his machine and then shouted at the other men coming toward the truck. "Yarda som apta gurta.

The men clustered around the giant and nodded. Their deference made it obvious that they considered him in control. They pushed buttons on a similar looking device, their brows furrowed in concentration. All of them had cuts and wounds, some even broken bones, but their focus was on the machine in their hand. Fiona had never seen anyone completely ignore what must have been huge physical pain. They needed immediate medical attention and her concerns forced her into action.

"We need to get help for these men." Fiona tried to push past the man still holding her door. Her fear was replaced by concern for the wounded.

"We take care of our own." The words were spoken with a faint accent, but the giant had definitely spoken English.

"Why didn't you speak English before?" Fiona didn't hide her exasperation. "They need hospitals and ambulances. Let me pass."

The man looked at her for a few seconds before giving her a slight bow of his head. "It is dangerous. I cannot guarantee your protection."

"Join the club." Fiona sarcastic tone elicited a raised eyebrow from the giant.

Let him wonder. No one had been able to protect her. That's why she was hiding in this remote area. She existed at the edge of life and society. That was better than the alternative, though.

"It is my sworn duty to protect." The giant's voice was emotionless. "I do not understand what you mean by club."

Fiona frowned. Was he making fun of her? "You're not sworn to do anything for me. I can take care of myself. I have medical training and can help. Let me go."

He let go of the door so quickly that Fiona almost fell out of the truck. His hand steadied her and she did her best to ignore the jolt of electricity that seemed to leap between them. He was a man. No man could be trusted.

"Pardon, my lady." The man stepped aside to let her pass.

"My name is Fiona." Her words came out in a breathy whisper. The man was a throwback to a different century. No one was that formal anymore. "Where did you come from?"

"You wish me to call you by your name?"

"Of course. What is your name?"

"I am Ardal." Again the man gave a slight bow of his head. "My men are at your service."

"I don't think they can serve anyone in their condition." Fiona turned to the men gathered around her vehicle. "I can start taking some back to my house and from there we'll call an ambulance."

"Jehon, start loading the men onto this vehicle and see if you can make it run." Ardal barked out the order. Immediately another large man jumped into her truck. Other men limped toward the rear and pulled themselves up as best they could.

"You can't just take my truck."

Fiona's protest was ignored. Instead they walked past her with their eyes lowered. It was the strangest group of men she'd ever encountered. They treated her with deference, but still ignored her words. Fiona started to go to the vehicle, but Ardal touched her arm. Again the jolt of electricity shot through her. She inhaled sharply, but kept her face impassive.

"Jehon can make any machine sing for him. If you will tell him the direction of your house he can take these men there before coming back for the rest.

Fiona bit her lip. What choice did she have? She was outnumbered. Maybe it was best for her to stay and help the rest of the survivors. She nodded and pointed in the direction of her house before walking toward the wreckage.

"You do me honor by agreeing to my advice." Ardal's voice was a low whisper. "I thank you Fiona, as do my men.

"Are you soldiers?" That had to be the explanation for the uniform and air of command. Except this group of men weren't like any military people Fiona had seen before.

"We are Hunters; elite warriors born and bred." There was a note of pride in Ardal's voice.

"Was it a secret mission, or will your people be sending out a search party?"

"What is the meaning of a search party?"

"You know, others sent to find you."

Ardal shook his head. "We are the last. No one will look for us."

"That's sad." Fiona's voice faded away. She had reached the first of the wounded. It was a young man, perhaps in his early twenties. His body was ripped open in several spots with bits of metal mixed in with the carnage.

Fiona knelt and examined him with experienced fingers. The most serious injury was a knife-shaped piece of metal protruding from his left thigh. That would require surgery before it was removed. She daren't risk taking it out now in case the man bled to death. Right now the metal was preventing anything serious from happening.

"This man needs immediate attention. We'll pack something around the metal so that it doesn't dislodge."

Ardal grunted his agreement. "Firbin is tough." He looked up at another man running toward him. "Get me a dressing."

Within seconds the material arrived. Fiona went to pack the wound, but Ardal stopped her. He put the small device he had shoved in her face to Firbin's leg and ran it over the skin. Then he gripped the metal and pulled it out. He was so quick that Fiona didn't have a chance to stop him. There was no blood, though. The metal hadn't been in a major artery. With a sigh of relief she sat back on her heels and watched Ardal's expert hands wrap a cloth-like material around the wound. When he was done, he opened his eyes and gave Ardal a crooked smile.

"Many thanks."

Ardal grabbed his hand. "Be strong. Remember you are a Hunter true and right."

The man nodded and closed his eyes on a sigh. Despite the strangeness of the words they seemed to comfort the man. Fiona glanced at the giant beside her. His face showed no expression, but his eyes burned with unmistakeable pride. It was obvious he cared about this man and the others. He was a puzzle. He was unlike any man she had met before.

Ardal stood and offered his hand. She grabbed it and went onto the next man. There was no hope for him. There was a huge gash in his chest, the organs beneath exposed to the air. His heart was torn and was pumping blood out with each beat. His life force was fading. Ardal knelt beside him, clasped his hand and bent to whisper in his ear. Fiona couldn't hear the words, but she noticed a strange peace come into the man before death claimed him.

"He died with honor." Ardal's voice was low, his head bent as a shiver seemed to pass through his body.

"How can there be honor in dying?" Fiona had seen enough death to know that most people welcomed it as a relief from pain, or were just too weary to fight any longer. Honor didn't play a part of it.

"Honor is all a Hunter has." Ardal stood. "Death is our reward, but to die fighting brings honor."

"What century are you from?" Fiona had only heard words like this in historical fiction, never from a real person. "Were you fighting on the plane and that's why it crashed?"

"We refused to be led to our death."

Before Ardal could continue speaking another man rushed up to them. "The Captain lives."

"Bring him to me." Ardal was definitely in command. He straightened his shoulders and his mouth thinned with determination.

A slight man with brown hair was pushed toward them. Fiona gasped when she saw that he was walking with a limp. That didn't seem to matter to the two men who were leading him. Then again they were also walking with difficulty and their wounds looked more serious. One of the men had a large gash to his forehead and blood was dripping down his face. The other's arm was bent, which suggested it was broken, on top of several gashes. Overall the man they led seemed to have gotten off light.

"Captain, you have earned honor." Ardal's voice was low with the faint hint of sarcasm. "That is more than you deserve."

"You were the ones who forced the ship down. If you had followed orders, none of this would have happened." The Captain shook off the hands of the two men holding him. "Your death would have ensured peace. They will hunt you down until every last one of you is dead."

"I think it is unlikely that the Holman will search for us. We are all dead to them." Ardal's tone was matter of fact, his features betraying no emotion.

"You killed all of my men." The Captain pushed forward and jabbed Ardal in the chest. "You're no better than animals."

"Because I refused to let my men be killed without honor?" Ardal shook his head. "We had no choice but to fight you."

"So you caused more loss. Hasn't there been enough death on our planet?" The Captain turned and gestured to the carnage all around them. "Look what you have done. Instead of dying, you will have to live with being traitors."

Fiona listened to this conversation with growing confusion. These men spoke in riddles. It sounded as if they had just come from a war, but that wasn't possible. The Middle East was the nearest battlefield. These men didn't look as if they came from there.

"Could one of you please explain where the hell you're from?"

The Captain and Ardal both turned to look at her. The Captain's eyes scanned her face and then perused her body with a lazy indolence that she had come to recognize. A shudder of revulsion skittered along her back. It was only then that she realized that Ardal and his men had not looked at her with lust.

"Ah, a beautiful mistress to greet us," the Captain said in a low voice. "This does look promising."

Fiona didn't have a chance to reply before Ardal had grabbed the man by the neck and lifted him from the ground. "You will be respectful in a woman's presence," he ground out between clenched teeth. He gave him a shake and then threw the man to the ground.

"My pardon, Fiona. The Captain forgets the rules of the Sacred Code. His actions suggest that he never knew them."

"You haven't answered her question." The Captain rubbed his neck and shook off the hands of the men trying to help him stand. "She has a right to know that you are traitors who have escaped from the Holman forces."

Fiona frowned. "I've never heard of them. Is that a country in Africa?"

The Captain snorted. "Look closely at my ruined craft and you'll see that it is beyond the technology of your people. We come from another planet."

Chapter 3

Traitors.

Another planet.

The words kept repeating in Fiona's head all that long night. When daylight had finally relieved the darkness, she had driven out to the far field where the crash had happened. What the night had hidden was now all too apparent. The Captain had not lied. The ruined hull of his craft was not a plane. It wasn't even like any of the experimental crafts she had seen on television. This was a large rounded vessel made from some sort of metal that glinted with a silver shimmer.

"Aliens."

Fiona whispered the word beneath her breath. Her mind shied away from such a thought. There was no such thing as aliens. Only crazy people believed in them. Insane headlines from some of the more disreputable magazines flashed through her head. It couldn't be possible that those lunatics had been telling the truth.

And if aliens were real, why would they come to earth?

The Captain had said that they came here to die. But there had to be a zillion better places in the universe to die. Earth was just another planet in a long line of them. No, there had to be another explanation. Perhaps they had gone off course. There had been a fight after all. That could be the only explanation.

But these men looked human. They were tall, all of them over six feet. Ardal had to be six seven at the very least, but it wasn't unheard of for men to be that tall. They seemed to have the same organs as humans. She'd helped with their medical care all last night. There were no visible differences. Perhaps at a cellular level there were variances, but nothing evident to the eye.

The only one that was different was the Captain. He was smaller, both in height and stature. He was probably no taller than five feet and slight build. If he had muscles, they didn't show under his clothing. The unusual thing about him was the shape and size of his eyes, nose, and mouth, and his lack of facial hair. His skin was smooth and without wrinkles. It was also a sickly pale color as if he had never seen the light of day.

Fiona heaved a sigh and walked back to her truck. There was no point in denying what had happened. A spacecraft had crashed in her back field. Her field was littered with debris and among the wreckage there were many more bodies. She had a houseful of male aliens. Most were wounded, but not severely. Ardal was already rounding up men to bury the dead. At least the evidence would be gone.

What was she thinking?

When had she accepted the impossible?

Sometime between last night and this morning her universe had been turned upside down. Thoughts of the men in black paying her a visit flittered through her mind. If the stories about aliens were true, then the rest of it must be true also. That meant a government cover-up of huge proportions. The only thing that was saving her from a full scale invasion of the military was the fact that she was in such a remote area. Perhaps no one had noticed a large alien spacecraft invading their airspace and crashing.

And pigs could fly.

Fear gripped her stomach. The problem of cleaning the devastation in her fields was the least of her worries. The publicity involved with an alien spacecraft in her back forty acres was something that she could do without. Her cover would be blown. David would find her all too soon, and then she'd be on the run again.

If he didn't catch her first.

Fiona shivered and brought her clenched hand up to her chest. The last time he'd almost killed her. If she hadn't pretended to be unconscious, he probably would have. She'd been lucky to escape. There was no way she was going to let it happen again. She had to protect her new identity and if necessary, she'd disappear again.

First she needed to take care of all the wounded aliens. Fiona shook her head and got into the truck. She had about one hundred and fifty men divided between her house and the barn. Most had injuries that needed attention, but Ardal had been serious when he'd said they look after their own. So far she'd only been allowed to do basic first-aid.

These men were more skilled than some surgeons Fiona had seen at the hospital that she'd interned at. They worked with swift, deft motions almost as if they knew intrinsically what the other man was feeling. They were like computers, moving quickly and without emotion. It was uncanny.

Fiona started the truck and smothered a yawn. She needed sleep. She put the truck in gear and headed back to the house. There was no point in delaying the inevitable. Somehow she needed a plan to deal with this situation and the possible consequences.

Confusion still reigned at the house. Men were everywhere. When she walked into the living room the men's voices stopped, though. Those who could stand did so. A surge of embarrassment rushed through her. She had never been treated with gallantry before. She thought that had gone the way of the dodo.

"Finally." The Captain's voice broke the spell. "You're a breath of fresh air. I'd never tire of looking at you, gorgeous."

Ardal's fist shot out and connected with Eamon's jaw, sending the man back against the couch. "Silence. By Cygnus and Warrior, you will learn respect."

Fiona cringed at the violence, but couldn't prevent an upwelling of thankfulness. She hated the sexual innuendos that she'd endured since she'd turned sixteen. It was a relief to know that these men would not step over the line.

"I've been out at the field. It's a bigger mess than I realized. I don't know how we're going to clean it up. The trees will take years to recover."

"We will cover the damage."

"How?" Fiona sank onto a kitchen chair. "You'd need big equipment to drag all the debris away."

"We are many." Ardal waved to his men. "We are used to cleaning up messes."

"The men need time to heal."

"There is no time." Ardal put his hands on his hips. "We heal fast."

"There's another thing." Fiona glanced back at the kitchen. It was a typically large farm kitchen, but she wasn't a big eater. "I don't have enough food for everyone. I'll have to go into town for groceries."

"We will find food." Ardal nodded to three of his men who moved forward. "Do you have any weapons?"

"There's a shotgun in the closet, but it's locked."

The men went for the gun and came back a few seconds later. "Can you work it?"

"It is primitive, but will be effective," the man holding the gun answered. "We will be back shortly."

"You're going to kill breakfast?" Fiona shook her head. Why not? They seemed to take care of everything else. She was too tired to care. "I need to sleep."

Anxiety and tiredness were catching up. She couldn't think properly especially with so many men surrounding her. Usually it only took one man to send her body into full panic. Now she was on overload. The fact that these guys kept their distance was the only thing making it bearable.

"Which is your sleeping chamber?" Ardal held his hand out to her.

Now that daylight had come, she could see that his hair was a deep dark brown, almost black. It was only the odd highlight that kept it from being black. His skin was olive-toned and his eyes a dark obsidian. He wasn't exactly a handsome man, but his air of command meant that he would never be overlooked in a crowd. Strangely enough, most of his men had almost the same dark appearance. The only one that was different was the pilot with his light brown hair.

Fiona took Ardal's hand, suppressing a gasp at the now familiar jolt that ran through her body when he touched her. She pointed to the room farthest away. "I can sleep somewhere else, though. I don't want to disturb those men. They need to recover. I just need to get my sleeping bag from the closet and then I'll sleep in my truck."

"No." He motioned to a couple of men. Before she could stop him, her bedroom had been cleared.

"Sleep." He led her to the room. "We need your truck to clean up the debris and bury our comrades. All will be taken care of by the time you waken."

Fiona knew it was useless to argue with the man. No matter how much she wanted to help, last night he'd pushed her aside. His only explanation was that it was not the work a woman need do. Doubtless things were different where he came from, but surely women worked there. She was too tired to think about it. Instead she snuggled into her bed and fell asleep.

She was a strange lady. Never had he seen such an exquisite female before and he had seen many an attractive mistress. The women on his planet were noted for their loveliness and grace, but none could compare with Fiona. Her hair was the color of the early morning dawn on his home planet, deep, rich red with a hint of gold. The people of his planet were either dark haired warriors or had hair the color of the Kaladin and their mates, which was brown.

The other difference was her eyes. They were a deep green, the shade of grass under the light of the setting sun. Her hair and eyes were truly spectacular, but even more so against the pale ivory of her skin. A creature of unique beauty, but never before had he seen such fear in a woman's eyes. She tried to hide it, but every time she looked at one of the men, it was there.

Despite this, she had insisted on helping. She looked fragile, but that was not the case. There was courage and strength in all her actions. He respected that, and even though it wasn't required of a warrior to admire those he obeyed, it would be an honor to serve her.

Ardal watched her enter her sleeping chamber before turning back to his men. The Captain was rubbing his jaw and glaring at him with hatred. He was less than a man. He would deal with him shortly.

As for the others, he had to ensure that their entry into this planet was hidden. That was his first task.

Ardal signaled Darrogh and Jehon. Garguin had died in the crash. Now Darrogh was next in command. The man was strong and loyal. He was a Hunter to be trusted. Jehon followed.

"We need to make the crash disappear." Ardal spoke low so Eamon could not hear. Then he turned his back on the Captain and continued to speak through mental connection. *"The Captain needs to be in a secure place where he cannot harm us."*

"There are slots in the barn." Darrogh was clearly amused. *"I believe they have been used for animals in the past."*

Ardal gave his second in command a steady gaze before nodding his affirmative. Eamon had to be dealt with and if it gave the men a bit of fun, so be it. The man might be able to give them information as to why they were being brought to this planet. If not, they would kill him.

"Can you run the equipment, Jehon?"

"It is primitive, but useable." Jehon stood with his feet apart, his body ready to obey. *"There is a machine that has been used to turn the fields. I think I can convert it to something that will dig."*

"Set as many men to the task that are able-bodied. I need the craft hidden and the bodies of our brothers and of our enemies buried or burned. Keep them separate."

"It can be no other way." Jehon nodded and then turned. Half of the less injured men followed.

Now it was the Captain's turn. Both he and Darrogh turned to the man.

"What?" the Captain whined. "Haven't you done me enough damage?"

"You are indiscreet and forget your place."

"We're not on Cygnus now. Women do not rule us here."

"That is no excuse for forgetting your breeding and rank." Ardal pulled the man to his feet. "By Cygnus and Warrior you will learn respect or die."

They dragged the Captain from the house and went to the barn. Already the log outbuilding was empty. The men residing there had followed Jehon.

There were numerous compartments in the building and Ardal chose one without a window. There would be no sunlight, but he could not risk him revealing their secrets.

"You can't leave me here."

Ardal slammed the compartment door shut and then used a chain to secure it in place. "We have no choice. Until I know we are safe, you must remain here."

"Don't think I'll keep quiet." The Captain raised his voice. "I'll bellow my innocence until someone comes to rescue me."

"So be it." Ardal unchained and opened the door. Darrogh pulled a syringe from his pocket and forced Eamon back against the wall. The Captain struggled, but to no avail. Darrogh injected the man and then watched him slowly slide down the wall of the barn. Within seconds he was sleeping on the pile of hay used as bedding.

"He will be silent for at least twelve hours."

Ardal nodded. "When he wakes, feed him and then inject him again. If he continues to be difficult, kill him. Without a craft to fly, he is not necessary. He may have information we need, but we cannot trust that he will not turn the people from this planet against us."

They left the barn and headed toward the far field where the crash had happened. The sun of this planet had risen less than an hour ago and with it a mist had formed over the land. It was a crisp, cool sensation. He had always preferred the cold to the heat of the palaces of the Kaladin.

That was the past.

They were on a new planet and must make a home for themselves. Once the evidence of their landing was hidden, he would decide what was best for him and his men. They were the last of the Hunter brotherhood. They must continue to survive until the Kaladin of Cygnus return to their rightful place as rulers.

They reached the crash site, which was hidden from the house. His men had been busy cleaning the area. They had gathered the dead into two separate funeral pyres. There was another pile of clothing, tools, and weapons that could be salvaged. Ardal reached in and pulled out a shirt to replace his torn one. After he'd changed, he walked to Jehon who held a burning torch out to him.

The first pyre held his fallen men. His body tensed as he forced his emotions under control. The loss of so many men at once was unheard of for Hunters. They lived every day knowing that death was their partner. To accept his own end was different than knowing his orders had led to the demise of others. He had less than a unit of men left. His hand tightened on the torch.

"They died with dignity." Darrogh's voice was low. "You have always led us true and right."

Ardal swallowed hard and straightened his shoulders. As their leader, he had one last duty. He would see their death had not been in vain. He walked to his fallen men and held the torch above his head.

"We do honor to our brothers who have died with courage." He lowered the torch to the pyre and watched as the flames began to lick through the bodies of the fallen. "Hunters true and right, their memory and deeds will remain with us until the end of time."

The fire burned quick. When it was finished the ashes were buried. Only then did Ardal move to the smaller second pyre of fallen Holman soldiers. Most had been disintegrated on entry to this planet, but a few of the dead still needed to be disposed of. He lit the fire and walked away.

The pieces of the spacecraft had been gathered in the area where the partially intact launching chamber had landed. Anything useable had been taken out. All that remained was the debris and shell of the craft. Ardal nodded and his order to destroy the craft was carried out. Within seconds it burst into a non-flammable explosion that consumed and melted the craft into globular fragments of shiny material. As soon as the reaction had finished, the pieces were scraped from the soil and buried.

With the site cleared of evidence all that remained was for the men to search the rest of the wooded area for pieces that may have been overlooked. He was about to join the search himself when a shout in his head stopped him. It was Firbin.

"*We have been found.*"

Chapter 4

Fiona awoke to the sound of loud pounding. At first she thought it was her head, but when men's voices were added to the noise, she knew there was someone at the front door. How could they have locked themselves out? If they were skilled enough to fly in space, they must know how to use a key.

With a groan she pushed away her blankets and stood. She still wore the clothes from the night before, wrinkled but presentable. She pulled her hair into a ponytail and went into the hall. She frowned when she entered the living room. It wasn't empty. The more severely wounded men were standing and alert. Who was hammering at the door?

Firbin was at her side before she reached the entryway. Despite his leg wound, he moved with a swiftness that Fiona had seldom seen before. Most men would be under sedation. His pain threshold had to be very different from humans.

"I'm coming." Fiona's voice was loud enough to carry through the door. She reached to open it when Firbin put a hand out to stop her. He shook his head once and she knew it wasn't the crash survivors. This was someone else.

Immediate fear coursed through her veins. David couldn't have found her. Beatrice, her contact at the Woman's Underground Network was the only person who knew where she was. She'd been warned that most women were found within a couple of years, but she'd been careful.

Her hand trembled as she grasped the handle. "Who is it?"

"It's Marshall, your neighbor down the road." The familiar voice filtered through the door. "I've got Clyde with me and we're hoping to have a look at your back field."

Fiona straightened her shirt. This could mean only one thing. Someone had seen the crash last night. She looked at Firbin, who nodded. She stepped outside and closed the door behind her. She never let anyone into the house.

"Isn't it a bit early for hunting season?" Fiona kept her voice light. "You don't need to set up another blind?"

Marshall was a small round man. He was in his late forties and had lived in the area his whole life. He gave her a crooked smile and a wink. Most of the man's teeth were yellow with nicotine stains and he was almost bald. Still, he seemed to think he was God's gift to women. There was no understanding the male ego.

"Nah, me and Clyde here just want to ask if you had anything strange happen. Clyde thinks he saw something fall out of the sky last night."

"Was it a meteor? I was in the fields last night watching the light show. It was quite spectacular. I would have noticed something fall, though."

Clyde leaned forward, his voice low. "I think it was one of those government planes. You know, the CIA or something like that."

"What would the CIA want with us?" Fiona bit back a smile. These guys had definitely watched too many conspiracy shows.

"They've secret airports around these parts." Clyde looked at Marshall. "Tell her."

"The CIA's been using this area for years. A cousin of mine works at an airport and he says they're always flying in low and saying their flight plan is classified."

"So you think they've crashed?"

Fiona looked back toward her fields. How long had Ardal and his men been working? She glanced up to the sun which was past the midday point. It was probably early afternoon. It would take days to clean up the mess, though. She couldn't risk letting these guys look at the field today.

"That's the most likely thing." Clyde shrugged. "The fireball was too big to be a meteor."

"Wouldn't the government be all over this by now?" Fiona's tone was doubtful. "I don't think they'd want a plane of theirs falling into the wrong hands."

Marshall cleared his throat. "We were thinking they don't know exactly where the crash site is."

"And you want to tell them?" Fiona didn't bother to hide her disbelief.

"There might be a reward." Clyde's voice was a low whisper. "Of course we'd cut you in for a bit of the money."

"Why would they give a reward?" Fiona tilted her head. "They're more likely to make you disappear."

Marshall swallowed hard and looked at Clyde. "We hadn't thought of that."

Clyde frowned and then shook his head. "If all we did was report it, I'm sure they'd leave us be."

"Why report it then?"

Fiona was searching for any excuse to make these men leave. She didn't owe her guests loyalty, but she didn't want them tracked down like dogs. That's what would happen if people knew that there were aliens among us. There'd be no safe place to hide. She wouldn't wish that experience on her worse enemy.

"Aren't you curious?" Marshall spat on the ground. "Hell I know you're new to these parts, but nothing interesting ever happens. This might be a chance to put Limer on the map."

Horror at the thought sent her heart into a pounding frenzy. Publicity was the last thing she wanted. She didn't need reporters or strangers poking around in her life, or her home. Fiona fought back her panic and tried to focus. The fear was paralysing, but she had to push past it and think. There must be a solution.

"Do we have to look today?" Fiona asked. "I was up all night watching the stars. Surely you guys could come back another time?"

"We understand." Marshall and Clyde looked at each other and moved away from her. "You go back to bed and we'll take a quick look at your field."

"No." Fiona shouted. She wanted these men gone, not giving her sympathy. "I don't want anyone on my property."

Clyde tilted his head. "Now that's a bit strange." His voice was a low growl. "You got something you're hiding back there?"

"Of course not." Fiona clasped her hands together. This was going from bad to worse. Now they were suspicious.

"Can I help you men?" Ardal's voice boomed in the distance.

Fiona's head jerked toward the barn. Never had she been so glad to see a man before. He was striding toward them, his steps purposeful and strong. Gone was the ripped and burned top of his uniform. In its place was a shirt that molded his body and showcased his powerful muscles. He wore fatigue styled pants and boots that looked heavy, but were silent with each step. The sun was behind him. It illuminated him in a soft glow, like an angel from a renaissance painting. Right now that was exactly what he was.

A saviour.

Somehow he'd known she needed help.

"Who are you?" Marshall's voice held a hint of speculation. "I knew Fiona couldn't be the goody two shoes she pretended to be."

Ardal stopped a foot away from Marshal and lifted an eyebrow. "What do you mean?"

Clyde snorted. "She acts like she's better than us, but I can see it just took the right kind of man to make her human."

Fiona's stomach tightened with revulsion. "He's a friend." Her voice shook with indignation.

Ardal glanced at her and then back at the men. "You have upset Fiona."

Marshall shrugged. "Look, between us men I'm glad for you. I've never seen a better looking woman. If you can get it on with her, hey I'm all for it."

Ardal's eyes narrowed. "Explain."

Clyde moved his hips in a crude imitation of the sexual act. Before he could repeat it, Ardal picked him up by his shirt and threw him on the ground. "Your suggestion is wrong."

Marshall put up his hands and backed away. "Hey man, we just assumed because you were here," his words petered out under the steely glare of Ardal's eyes.

"Only stupid men make assumptions." Ardal moved toward the second man.

Fiona put her hand on his arm to stop him. Again that strange sensation of electricity rushed through her body, causing her breath to catch in her throat. Was this the way it was with all aliens? Did they have an energy field around them that affected humans? Fiona shook off the thought and focused on the problem before her.

"These men want to check out the back field." Fiona forced a smile. "They think they saw something fall from the sky last night."

He turned back to the men. "Which field?"

Marshall pointed to the one furthest away and closest to the forest. Ardal nodded and walked toward it. Clyde stood and followed, motioning Marshal to come too. Was the man insane? Fiona ran to catch up with them. If there was going to be a scene, she was damn sure she'd be part of it.

Reaching the field was anticlimactic.

Instead of a wrecked spacecraft, there was newly tilled soil. All evidence was gone. Fiona glanced at Ardal, but his stony face gave nothing away. His men must have worked miracles to have the crash debris and bodies cleared up this fast.

"So this is why you needed a man around." Clyde spoke in a subdued voice. "I didn't know you were interested in farming."

Fiona shrugged. "I just want to maintain the land. The bush was starting to encroach. Before long it would have reverted back to nature."

"Most of these fields do." Marshall bent down and picked up a handful of dirt. "The soil's too poor to support much but trees. Still, it's a shame to think of all the work it took to clear it going for naught."

"I want to look into the bush." Clyde started walking toward the trees. "If it isn't in the open, then the forest is a good place for it to be."

Ardal nodded. "How far do you intend to search?

"Just a few feet," Clyde said with a raised eyebrow. "I'm trying to satisfy my curiosity."

"You know what they say about curiosity." Fiona's tone was teasing. "I'd hate that to happen to you gentlemen."

"That sounded like a warning." Marshall was suddenly too close.

Fiona stepped back, but bumped into Ardal. He pushed her behind him. She found herself staring at the back of his shirt. The man was huge. She tried to look around him, but his hands prevented her.

"I never make threats." Ardal crossed his arms over his chest. "Take your look and then leave Fiona's property."

"Come on Marshall." Clyde was already at the edge of the bush. "We don't have all day."

Marshall gave Ardal an uncertain look and then followed his friend. When they were out of earshot, Fiona stepped from around Ardal.

"Will they find anything?"

Ardal shrugged. "If they go too far my men will kill them."

"No." Fiona's voice rose. She clapped her hand over her mouth when she saw Marshall look back at her. "Sorry," she whispered.

"My men have their orders."

"You can't go around killing people." Fiona forced her voice to stay low. "We have laws in this country."

"I will not risk my men's lives." Ardal's voice was firm. "There is less than a unit of Hunters left in the universe. It is my responsibility that they live."

Fiona frowned. "Are you saying that you and your men are all that's left?"

"Yes."

Fiona swallowed. Ardal's expression had not changed, but a flicker of intensity flashed into his black eyes before he hid it. Despite his appearance of control and dispassion, this man felt deeply about his responsibility. She'd been wrong to think him a computer on steroids. He cared about his men. You just had to dig deep to find it.

Before she could think of something to say, Marshall shouted at them. "It looks as if some of these trees have been cut down."

"I have a right to heat my house." Fiona didn't try to hide her exasperation. How dare these men come onto her land and interrogate her. For a second, she forgot that all she wanted was to lie low and avoid conflict. "Do I come onto your property and question what you do?

"Whoa." Clyde held up his hands. The men were walking back now. "We're just asking."

"I'll bet," Fiona hissed under her breath. Louder she said, "Do you want to see my woodpile? I could use help stacking it."

"You have a fine strong man to do that." Marshall glanced at Ardal and then cleared his throat. "I mean, we'll be happy to help, but it looks like you have everything under control."

"I do." Fiona straightened her shoulders. "I hope that you're satisfied that nothing fell on my land."

"We're just doing our civic duty." Clyde smirked. "I wouldn't want to have little green men roaming freely around these hills."

Fiona snorted. "You have a vivid imagination."

They walked back to the driveway. Once the men were on their way, Fiona turned to Ardal.

"We have to talk."

"I am at your service."

At the house Firbin was still standing guard, but a nod from Ardal and he was gone. The living room was full of men. The only private space was Fiona's bedroom. It wasn't ideal for a discussion, but what other choice was there? Taking a deep breath, Fiona went to her room and waited for Ardal to follow her in before closing the door.

She leaned her back against the door. It was time she knew exactly who her guests were. "Where are you and your men from?"

"Our planet is Cygnus. It is in what we call the Zonar galaxy."

"How far is it from Earth?"

"What is earth?"

"That's the planet that you're on, Earth." Fiona let out a sigh. "It seems that we're talking different languages."

"We are."

Ardal put his hand on her arm and led her to the bed. Again the jolt of electricity ran through her body. Fiona looked into Ardal's eyes, but he seemed unaware of the sensation. Instead he pressed her onto the bed and then stood in front of her, arms crossed and legs apart.

"I do not know the distance we traveled before reaching your planet. We were on the spacecraft for several months."

"I can't think with you looming over me." Fiona motioned to the chair in the corner of the room. "Sit. I need to understand who you are."

Ardal made a grunting noise and took the seat. "What questions do you have?"

"Are you a criminal?"

"Do you mean did I break the Sacred Code?" Ardal lips tightened. "Yes."

Now she was harboring criminals. Judging by his behavior, they were probably murderers. She glanced at the closed door. Perhaps a private meeting wasn't her most brilliant idea.

"We did not harm anyone." Ardal's words forced Fiona to look at him. "We refused to obey the order that would have executed us."

Fiona bit her lip. "Usually you do something bad before you get executed. What did you and your men do?"

"We followed our orders."

Fiona pursed her lips and bit back her exasperation. The man couldn't answer a simple question. "You said you didn't follow orders."

"We followed the orders of the Kaladin."

Fiona shut her eyes for a second. This was going nowhere. She glanced up at the peeling paint of her ceiling and decided to try a different direction. "The Captain called you traitors."

"The Captain is an instrument of the Holman. He believes Hunters should no longer exist." Ardal leaned forward, his eyes intent on Fiona. "The Holman won the civil war on my planet. They defeated the Kaladin and now control all of Cygnus and its territories.

"So you lost the war?"

The muscles in Ardal's jaw tightened. "A Hunter does not lose. We were forced to obey a dishonorable order."

Fiona sighed. It was like talking in circles. "What exactly does a Hunter do?"

"We are a race of our own, the elite of the warriors."

"So you are soldiers." She'd been right about their military look.

"We are more than that." Ardal's voice held pride. "A Hunter lives and dies by honor. We search and we destroy. We obey only the orders of the Kaladin and we defend to the death."

Fiona frowned. It sounded like something out of the middle ages. It had to be a matter of the language barrier because their technology was way beyond the middle ages. Weren't advance races supposed to be peaceful? At least that's what all the science fiction shows portrayed.

"So you lost the war and were ordered executed. That seems an extreme action. Why wouldn't the new leaders just use you to help them?"

"They knew we would never give them our loyalty. We have been bred to obey the Kaladin. We would die to keep them safe."

"But the Kaladin are gone now, so where does that leave you."

Ardal hesitated for a fraction of a second. "The Kaladin high council survives."

Fiona looked at Ardal's closed face and instantly knew. "You and your men saved them."

"It was our last order."

"And that order led you to be executed."

Ardal shook his head. "No. All other Hunters were executed. I chose to fight."

"So that was what the Captain meant when he said you had caused the ship to crash."

"The Captain fired a weapon at the guidance computers and that caused our crash."

Fiona rolled her eyes. She had only met this guy last night, but she knew enough to believe he'd provoked it. "You had something to do with that, though."

"I asked him to drop his weapon."

"I'm sure you were polite about it."

"There was no need for politeness. It was a battle."

"I was being sarcastic. Don't they have sarcasm on your planet?"

"We speak only what we mean."

"Nice to know," Fiona said under her breath. In a louder tone she asked. "What happens now?"

"We cannot stay. The spacecraft was destroyed, so we will have to build another."

Fiona stood. "People would notice that. You don't want to be hunted down by the authorities. I know what that feels like."

"You are hunted?"

Fiona picked up the brush from her dresser and began to tap it against her palm. How much information was it safe to give this guy? What difference did it make, though? They would be gone soon and she'd be safe again.

"A man is stalking me." Fiona motioned to the window. "That's why I'm hiding in the middle of nowhere."

Ardal gave her a steady look. "Is it not wrong for him to do this?"

"If a man wants to kill you, he will. There's nothing the law can do to stop it." Fiona let out an exasperated breath. "I'd fallen completely off the grid and then this happens. We'll be lucky if the military aren't all over this thing."

"They are already searching."

Chapter 5

"You can't know that for certain." She looked at Ardal to see if he'd been trying to scare her, but his face was serious. That meant her cover was blown. Clyde and Marshall were just the start. She dropped onto the bed.

"Your technology is advanced enough to know that we crashed." Ardal shifted in the chair.

"That's doesn't mean they're looking for you."

"The scanners suggest otherwise."

Fiona frowned. "I don't have the internet much less a radio scanner."

Ardal held up the device he had pushed into her face the night before. She'd thought it was a phone. Obviously it was much more, probably a mini-computer or something. It was definitely evidence of the advanced technology that Ardal and his men must have access to. What else were they hiding? Did it matter, though? Soon she'd be on the run again. First, she had to deal with the injured men.

Fiona straightened her shoulders. "We have to get you and your men hidden. It's been over twelve hours since you landed. Soon the military and police will have narrowed their search. If Clyde and Marshall saw something, you can believe others did."

"We hit something upon entry. Half of our craft was missing when we cleaned up." Ardal's voice was matter of fact. "There are two crash sites. They are wasting their time with the first site."

There was no point in speculating how he knew this. "How much time before they find you?"

"Two hours, maybe less."

Fiona bit her lip. She knew how to hide one person, but there were over one hundred men here, some with serious injuries. She only had the one vehicle and it held four in the cab. You might be able to squeeze another ten in the box, but that would get noticed on the highway.

"How do I hide so many?" Fiona whispered her thought aloud.

"You do not do anything." Ardal's voice was severe. "The site is cleaned and the evidence of our crash is gone. I have made plans for my men."

That left only her to worry about. Fiona's heart began to race. She had to make plans before the panic set in and made it impossible to think. She pushed her hair off her face. She had to hide. She had an emergency kit readied as she'd been trained. Now she needed to consider where to go.

"We will protect you." Ardal had left the chair and was now crouched in front of her. "You must not fear."

Fiona started to laugh, a hysterical, uncontrollable imitation of a laugh. "You can't protect me. Don't you understand?"

"We are Hunters. We can do many things."

"I'm sure you can, but you don't know David."

Flashes of memory flitted through her mind. He was one of the senior residents at the hospital where she had done her first internship. She had been flattered and naïve. Too many years of focusing on school had kept her isolated. She seldom dated and when David had first approached her, she had thought it was a fairy tale.

He was good looking and charming, but that had changed after the first couple of dates. He had been way too serious, demanding that she only see him. She had refused and said that she was too young. She had years of schooling ahead of her before she could consider a serious relationship.

That was the first time he had beat her.

She had barely escaped alive.

A gentle shake brought her out of her memories. Fiona shuddered, unable to focus on the man in front of her. "You can't know the horror of it."

"Tell me." His voice was a whisper.

"I fought him, but he was stronger. I couldn't escape. He took and took until there was nothing left of me. I'd rather die than go through that again."

"This monster still lives?"

Ardal's voice broke through her trance. "I'll have to contact the Women's Underground Network." Fiona stood up and started for the door. "The sooner I leave, the better chance I'll have of not being found."

Ardal's hand shot out and pressed against the door before she could open it. "We have caused this. We will fix it."

Fiona opened her mouth to protest when Ardal put his finger against her lips. The world went silent. There was only the two of them. Fiona usually shrank away from a man's touch, but instead of revulsion, she felt a strange comfort. A sense of belonging and safety seeped through every pore in her body.

"You are my responsibility now." Ardal's voice held a reverence, his words a vow. "I will protect you until my death."

Fiona couldn't tear her eyes away from his. There was a fire deep within, turning his obsidian eyes molten. Warmth filled her, releasing the tension of the last year of running. She believed him. He would protect her. She leaned into him.

"What happens when he finds me?"

"He will never touch you again." Ardal put his arms around her, hugging her close to his pounding heart.

No revulsion in this man's arms, only peace. Fiona shivered and pushed away. What was she thinking? She'd almost been lulled by the fairy tale again. They didn't exist. Ardal was a man, even if he was an alien. It was dangerous to let her defenses down around men.

"You do not trust yet." Ardal opened the door and let her pass through before him. "It must be earned."

The living room was a hive of activity. The men were up and moving, even the injured. "What's going on?"

"We are ready to leave."

Just like that. No goodbyes, no thank you. Her world was turned upside down and they were leaving. Fiona bit her lip and forced her voice to remain calm. "Where are you going?"

"We do not want the military to find us." Ardal nodded at a couple of the men who were handing out revolver-like weapons. "My men will disperse and when it is safe we will meet up again."

"How will you keep in touch?" Fiona walked over to the sideboard in her kitchen. "What about food. You haven't eaten anything since you arrived. Your men will need food to keep them healthy."

"We have eaten." One of Ardal's men gave him a small piece of meat and he handed it to her. "Here."

Fiona sniffed at it before putting it in her mouth. "Moose?"

"It was a large black animal." Ardal took another piece from his man and ate it before reaching into a bowl of berries and bringing some out to show Fiona. "Are these safe to eat."

Fiona took one from his hand and smiled. "These are blackberries. They are very safe and very good. You might have to fight off the bears for them, though."

"Describe bear."

"It's a big furry creature. Sometimes walks on two legs and loves berries." Fiona reached for more blackberries. "They'll attack, though."

"We are Hunters. No animal is a problem for us."

Fiona shrugged her shoulders. Let them find out for themselves that bears and wolves were not meant to be tangled with. She'd done her best to warn them.

"What are you planning?"

"We will walk out of this area."

Fiona choked on a berry that got caught in her throat when she'd started to laugh. "Do you know where you are?"

"No. Our guidance systems went down before the crash. Our individual instruments are unable to locate us." Ardal held up the small device. "Do your people have mapping systems?"

"We have maps. Do you want to see one?"

"It would be most useful."

Fiona went to the bookshelf and pulled out a small atlas and then a map of Ontario. She spread them on the kitchen table and the men gathered around. Ardal aimed his small device at the map she opened up and then clicked something.

She found Limer and pointed to it on the map. "This is us. We're about seventeen miles away from Wawa. That's the closest place for supplies."

"You drive there in your vehicle?"

"Yes." Fiona flipped the map and pointed to a more southerly area. "This is where most of the people live. You're lucky you didn't crash here. There would have been no hiding a UFO."

"What is that?"

"It's an unidentified flying object." Fiona gave him a crooked smile. "As crazy as it sounds, tons of people think that UFO's, or aliens are constantly visiting Earth."

"We have never been here before."

Fiona shrugged. "All I know is that a lot of people believe in these things and once there's a hint that one's crashed, they're all over it."

Ardal frowned. "Explain."

"It's not just the military you have to worry about. Ordinary people follow crashes of supposed spacecraft." Fiona shivered at the thought of crazy people in RV's roaming her fields, looking for evidence of extraterrestrial life forms. "It would be a nightmare.

Ardal crossed his arms over his chest. "Where is it best to hide?"

"I'd suggest someplace where you can blend in." Fiona moved her finger on the map until she'd reached its southerly point. "A large city like Toronto."

"How do we get there?"

"Driving is the only way." Fiona folded the map and opened the atlas to a map of the world. "You crashed in Canada." She pointed to the country and then her finger moved south. "This is the United

States. Right now, they're the most powerful nation in the world. You can bet that they know you're here."

"What will they do?"

"They'll destroy you." Fiona lowered her voice to a whisper. "They have a lot of advanced technology. If they think that you're a threat, they won't hesitate to cross the border."

"We are more advanced." Ardal's words were a statement. "We can evade them if we know what to anticipate."

"Expect mass hysteria if it ever comes out that you're from another planet." Fiona clasped her arms around her abdomen. "Most people don't believe in aliens."

"Believing has nothing to do with reality." Ardal looked at the map of the world. "Explain these areas."

Fiona gave him a quick version of world history. Ardal and his men were frowning when she'd finished. "What?"

"You have a violent history." There was no condemnation in Ardal's words. "We understand this."

"You mean because you're soldiers?"

"We are Hunters. We are the elite warriors." Pride shone through Ardal's words. "We are the ones sent in to fix the messes of others, or to make sure that nothing begins. We hunt and we kill."

"So you'll be at home here. Why doesn't that comfort me?"

She already lived in a world of chaos. She didn't want to think that she'd contributed to it becoming even crazier. What if they decided to go on a killing spree? If they were as deadly as they claimed, how many innocent humans would be killed? Protecting them might not be such a good idea.

"You worry we will be dangerous. There is no need. We fight with honor."

"How does that make a difference?"

"Most people fight to gain something, or for power. That is not our reason."

"It might be if you hope to live on this planet." Fiona's heart sank. These men would not last long without a means of support. How could they possibly blend into western society?

"We will find a way." Ardal motioned for his men to gather closer. "Our services are always needed."

"That's what I'm afraid of," Fiona muttered under her breath. She watched Ardal gather his men in groups of two and three before turning back to her.

"Is this city of Toronto a good place to meet together?"

"It's big enough that your men will get lost in the crowds." Fiona shrugged. "If you want true anonymity, then I would suggest a larger city in the United States like New York."

"We will gather in Toronto first." Ardal turned back to his men. "It is decided. I will give each of you a direction and you will follow that trail for a week, cover your tracks, and then turn south."

Fiona went and sat on the couch. There was no point in interfering with these men's plans. She had to make decisions about her own life. She'd put a call into the Women's Underground and ask advice. She couldn't risk David finding her. If she had to move on, so be it. She'd done it before. She could do it again.

Once Ardal left the house, she pulled out her emergency gear and rifled through it for her contact Beatrice's telephone number. There was no answer. She dialed the main office's number and again no answer, but this time an answering machine connected. She left a brief message about her situation, leaving out all details of the men who'd landed on her fields. She just said that there was probably going to be publicity in the area.

All that was left for her to do was wait.

Too nervous to sit, she cleaned up the evidence of her visitors. Still too restless to sit, she flicked on the radio. The announcer's voice shot through her like a knife.

"Giant fireball tracked over the northern skies last night."

Chapter 6

This planet, Earth, was similar to where he had been bred and trained, Beligia. It was an outer moon of a large planet in the same solar system as Cygnus. Cygnus was barren of trees and the atmosphere artificially maintained because it had been destroyed eons ago. Here each breath he took filled his lungs with energy. To gaze at the trees gave him joy. This would be a good planet to stay on.

Everywhere he looked there were lush greens and blue sky. Where the ship had crashed there had been a pond with clear water in it. Water had been one of the first things to be depleted after the ancient destructions. Now it was imported from other planets. To bathe in water was a luxury that only the elite of Cygnus were afforded. There weren't as many people here, either. That was a good thing. Fewer people meant fewer witnesses.

That meant less people to kill.

It was his duty to keep his men safe and Fiona protected. He had left her sitting on the couch, frowning. She did not believe he would protect her. In time, she would learn to trust the word of a Hunter. For now he must focus on his men.

"We need to disperse. Darrogh and his men have cleaned up the debris." Ardal handed the first group of Hunters his personal reader and they took the map from it and downloaded onto theirs before passing it to the others.

As the last man finished, Darrogh and his crew drove in from the field. They stood at attention and waited for Ardal's signal before giving their report.

"There was very little salvageable. We gathered the useable clothing and weapons."

Ardal pointed to the rear of the truck. "Each group take what you need. You have your orders. Firbin and Jehon stay with me."

They would obey. If there was a problem, they would contact him by mind connection. Each group left in a separate direction. Darrogh and his group of four were the last to leave. They were uninjured. Their mission was to head straight to Toronto in the hope that any search parties would follow them. That should give the others a better chance of survival. Once Darrogh's group was gone, he turned to Firbin and Jehon.

"We will be taking the woman with us." Ardal's voice was low. "We have put her life in danger. I promised her my protection."

Firbin and Jehon nodded their acceptance of his decision without question. There would be four of them traveling together. Firbin's injury and Fiona's inexperience would hinder their escape. Their one advantage was that the woman knew the people of this strange land. She could guide them if there was a problem.

Ardal took a look up at the sky. There was only one sun on this planet and it was well past the midpoint. They must start their journey soon. He glanced at the barn. He had one other thing to do.

The Captain must die.

At that moment Fiona walked out of the house. She glanced around and frowned back at him. For a second his mind froze as he gazed into her green eyes. Never had he found himself attracted to a woman. It was forbidden for a Hunter to mate. The Sacred Code was too ingrained for him to disobey, but still he could not deny that this woman affected him.

"Where are the men?"

"They have gone." Ardal waited for her reaction and wasn't disappointed. Her mouth dropped open and she ran down the driveway looking in all directions. In a couple of minutes she was satisfied that everyone had disappeared.

"Do they know where they're going?"

"They have their orders." Ardal took her arm and turned her back to the house. "Now we must clear up one last loose end."

Fiona dug her feet into the ground and refused to move. "What's that?" Her tone was suspicious. "Everyone is gone."

Ardal had never lied to a woman before and he would not start now. He remained silent instead. Jehon and Firbin kept their gazes on the ground. They knew what their next orders would be.

Fiona's eyes narrowed. "Your men are gone," she muttered under her breath. "Who else is there?" It took her a second before she shouted. "The Captain. Where is he?"

"In the barn." Ardal cleared his throat. "We had to persuade him to remain silent."

"Now you want to permanently silence him." Fiona tilted her head at him. "You're so transparent. You just kill everyone who gets in your way. I'm surprised you didn't kill me or am I next on your agenda?"

Ardal released her arm as if her words had burnt him. He stepped back. Shock and disappointment rocked through his body. Firbin and Jehon stiffened in revulsion. The air crackled with the horror of Fiona's suggestion. She seemed unaware of it though, as she stood glaring her defiance at them.

"Never," he swore. "That would be against the most sacred of our codes."

"Well I'm glad for that. How come the Captain doesn't fall into the same category?"

"He is the enemy." Ardal straightened his shoulders. "He is not a woman."

Fiona's face scrunched up. "That makes no sense."

"It is forbidden for a Hunter to kill or harm a woman or child. That is the first rule of our Sacred Code."

"You never disobey this code?" Fiona raised an eyebrow.

"It is what we live by." Ardal took her arm and led her back to the house. "We are wasting time by arguing. We should have started on our journey."

"Well you can go. Leave me with the Captain. I'm sure he'll be no problem, especially once I threaten him with the police."

"The man is dangerous." Ardal felt a familiar determination strengthen his muscles. "You are to come with us. I promised."

"Whoa, just a minute there. I don't need anyone else's help, especially not a man's." Fiona pulled away from Ardal and started to back up. "I have contacted the Women's Underground Network and they will place me again."

"There isn't time. Your military is within a couple of miles of finding us. We need to move now."

Ardal stood with his feet spread and arms crossed. "The decision has been made and you will come with us. Go and gather a small bag of necessary items. It would be good if you could bring the paper map also."

"Let the Captain live. Hasn't there been enough death." Fiona touched his crossed arms, her eyes looking up at him, pleading. "Besides, it will be the military who find him. They can decide what to do with him."

"He will give us away."

"Do you honestly think they'll believe what he says? They'll think he's a lunatic."

"So you want him left here for the others to find?"

"Yes." Fiona moved close enough that he could see the dark ring around the green of her eyes, "He won't know where you are, and you've covered up the debris, so anything he tells them will look like a lie."

"This is not a good decision." Ardal felt a tightening in his stomach. Years of training told him that leaving the Captain alive would only mean trouble later on. What was he to do though? If Fiona insisted he must obey. "He will hurt us in the future."

"If that happens then you can deal with him then. He's on a new planet, too. Give him a second chance to prove he's not a monster. Let him live."

"This is your order?"

"Yes."

Ardal glanced back at Firbin and Jehon. They both nodded their understanding. A Hunter would not leave the man alive. He knew too much and was dangerous. There was no arguing with a woman's instructions though, even if that woman was unfamiliar with the ways of war. She was not in direct harm, so there was no reason to countermand the order.

He stepped back. "As you wish. Now prepare your stuff. We leave in five minutes."

Fifteen minutes later, Ardal was pacing outside the house when he heard the distinct sound of a flying machine. He motioned his men into the house. It would be best not to be caught outside where they might be identified as strangers.

"Is that a helicopter?" Fiona rushed up from the lower level of her house. She carried an odd shaped pack that was stuffed full.

"Whatever it is, we must keep out of sight."

"That's for sure." Fiona dropped her sack at the door. "What if they have thermal imaging equipment?"

Ardal grunted. Why could this planet not be more primitive? It would make it easier to blend in. Thankfully his men were gone. A large group of Hunters would have been suspicious.

"What other ways do they have to detect people?"

Fiona frowned. "I know they have infrared stuff, night vision, and satellites that are orbiting the planet that can see you and hear you. They have to be in position though. As far as I know they can't see through walls."

"This is certain?"

Fiona shrugged. "That's what all the conspiracy shows say."

Ardal's eyes narrowed. "What is a conspiracy show?"

"It's when people start seeing the bogey man around every corner. They think that the government is lying to them, every news story is false, and little green men…" Fiona's voice trailed off.

"What?"

"…have landed on earth." Fiona looked at him with widened eyes. "They were telling the truth."

"What are green men?"

"Aliens." Fiona sank into a chair as if the life force had been drained from her. "People from other planets," she whispered.

Ardal fought the urge to reassure her. It was primitive in its intensity. He clenched his hands into fists and turned away. He must fight this connection with Fiona. It was unnatural for a Hunter to feel such things for a woman.

"So now you believe these things?" He forced the words through his clenched teeth.

Fiona sighed. "Obviously some of them are true." She stood and went to the window and craned her neck upwards. "It's definitely a helicopter and it's flying low."

"They are searching."

Fiona turned away from the window. "What do we do?"

"We stay put." Ardal gave his orders to his men through mind connection. "*Ready yourselves for battle.*"

"We can take the truck." Fiona went to the kitchen and poured water into a kettle. "At least we can make good time that way."

Ardal frowned. Once his men were in populated areas they would find transportation to get them to their destinations. Initially, he had planned the truck to remain here, but things had changed. The Captain would be left alive and that meant that he would have transportation when he escaped. No. The truck could not stay.

"We will take the truck as you suggest. That way the Captain will have to walk into the wilderness." Ardal allowed himself a half smile.

"You'd like that." Fiona shook her head and set the kettle on the stove. "You think he'll die."

"It would be best."

Fiona turned the burner on. "You have a devious mind."

"I am a Hunter."

Suddenly the house shook and the sound of propeller blades overhead made it too loud to think. Fiona put her hands over her ears. Ardal went to the window and watched the helicopter land on the field nearest the house.

They had visitors.

He motioned Jehon and Firbin into one of the back rooms and then shut the door. They had already played this game once with the neighbors, so it should not be too difficult. He touched Fiona's arm and pulled her behind him. If these men came in with weapons, then at least she would be safe.

The noise subsided to a low roar.

"We should go and meet them." Fiona's voice was a whisper. "Can they find anything?"

"No."

Ardal moved to open the door, but Fiona yelled "Wait."

She went to the stove and turned it off and then picked up her sack and threw it into a closet. She gave the room one last look before nodding. "I don't want to give them a reason to search the house."

Ardal sent a mental message to Jehon to do reconnaissance and then he focused all his energies on dealing with the situation outside. Fiona must not be hurt no matter the outcome. They would take out the men and the helicopter if need be.

He opened the door and grabbed Fiona's hand. He kept her at his side as they walked into the field. The long summer hay was being flattened by the rotating blades of the helicopter and he hesitated to go much closer. The blades started to slow down and the engine quietened just as the doors of the helicopter opened. Four men with guns stepped out.

"Crap." Fiona's hand tightened around Ardal's.

"There is no need to fear." Ardal eased himself in front of her. "These men can be handled."

"They have guns."

"So do I." He took a step toward the men. "Can we help you?"

The lead man ducked beneath the blades and walked toward them with his rifle resting across his arms. "We're looking for survivors from a plane crash."

Ardal relaxed the tension in his body. He forced his breathing and his heart rate to slow. He did not want these men to suspect anything. If he had to attack, he wanted the element of surprise on his side.

"We have seen no strangers here, unless you count the neighbors that came around earlier."

He felt Fiona move to his side. By Cygnus and Warrior if these men threatened her, he would have no recourse but to kill them. Jehon had better be in position.

"Did Marshall and Clyde send you here?" Her voice held a note of disgust. "I told them nothing had crashed last night. If it had, it was probably just a meteor or space junk."

"And you are?" The lead man's voice was devoid of expression.

"I live here." Fiona took a step forward before Ardal could stop her. "Who are you and what are you doing landing a helicopter on my property?"

"We aren't at liberty to discuss that with you."

Fiona crossed her arms. "Then I'm not at liberty to discuss anything with you."

Ardal inhaled deeply and banked back his irritation. Aggravating these men would only bring others. He held up his hands in a conciliatory motion. "They are only doing their job."

The first man seemed to relax a fraction. "We need to ask a few questions."

Fiona's eyes narrowed and then she threw up her arms. "Go ahead."

The lead man motioned for two of the others to follow him. Ardal led them away from the noisy helicopter and in the opposite direction. Jehon was good at blending in, but he didn't want to make it any more difficult for him.

"Why do you think a plane crashed here?" Ardal asked once they were out of earshot of the noisy blades.

"We don't." The man eased his rifle a bit lower in his arms. "There was a radar inconsistency and we sent out a plane to investigate and it disappeared."

"It disappeared here?" Fiona shook her head. "I would have heard something that loud."

"It happened during the night." The man turned unwavering eyes on Fiona. "It's possible that you were sleeping."

Fiona started to fidget under the man's gaze. Ardal cleared his throat and drew the man's attention back to him. The man was a trained soldier and he was suspicious. If he had to kill these men, more would follow. He dare not risk Fiona getting hurt.

"We will help you as much as possible."

The man raised one eyebrow. "We've already searched the property from the air. Now I want to look into the buildings. We'll start with the barn."

Chapter 7

"No." Fiona was too startled to stop her response. "You've no right to search here."

"We have whatever rights are deemed necessary."

"I don't even know who you are."

"I'm Captain Wilson. I have been assigned to search all the properties in the area. Your consent is not needed in this matter."

"So we're a military state now?" Fiona brushed aside Ardal's hand. "I'm sick of what you men decide is your right. I live a quiet life here. Then you come and start poking your noses where they don't belong."

"That's an interesting reaction." The man motioned his men to the barn. "What are you hiding?"

"Myself." Fiona fairly screamed the word. "I came here so I could be free of men who take what they have no right to."

Ardal's hand gave her back a tentative pat. He was trying to calm her, but she'd had enough. First, aliens crash and now the military wanted to search everywhere. It was too much to take. She'd been up all night, had only a couple hours of sleep, and now this. Everyone was poking their nose where it didn't belong. David would find her now. Tears started to prick her eyes and as hard as she tried, she couldn't stop them.

"She is overwrought."

Ardal squeezed her arm. His touch was gentle. His message was clear. She needed to get control of herself. That was easier said than done. She was making these men uncomfortable, but she didn't care. They'd turned her world upside down.

The soldier cleared his throat. "We have to ascertain that there is no one hiding here."

"I understand, but Fiona is in hiding from an abusive man." Ardal eased her closer to him. "Your helicopter and guns are upsetting her."

Fiona hiccupped and then turned to face the soldier. "I thought I'd be safe here and now you come and start threatening me."

"I apologise, ma'am." The soldier rocked on his feet. "If you let us check the buildings then we'll be able to move on. No one will disturb you again."

"Do you need to look in the house?" Ardal's voice was low.

The soldier hesitated for a second. "Yes."

"Do that first." Ardal's thumb moved in a soothing pattern on her arm. "Then I can take her there to calm down."

"Of course." The soldier whistled to his men and motioned them to the house.

Fiona wiped away her tears. What was Ardal thinking to let these men search the place? Ardal tightened his hold and instead of being uncomfortable, she felt safe. There was no point in fighting. If he didn't care, then why should she?

She sniffed. "I'm sorry, Captain." Her apology was met with a nod from the soldier.

"We'll be as quick as possible."

"You won't tell anyone about seeing me?"

"No ma'am." The Captain didn't blink an eye.

He lied like every other man she'd known. Everything that happened here would be in a report to some bigwig in the military. Did they think she was a fool? Still, what choice did she have? She turned her face into Ardal's chest and inhaled. The man smelled divine. She'd never noticed that about a man before. Maybe it was because he was from another planet.

Her mind skittered away from the direction it was going. It wasn't okay to be intrigued by this man. She knew better. Men only brought her grief and she'd had enough of that to last a lifetime. The sooner she found a new hiding place, the better.

She was overtired. That was the only explanation. She'd been running for over a year now without any hope of true safety. Surely her luck had to change soon.

"All clear."

The shout startled Fiona and she jumped. Ardal held her tight though, and somehow she sensed that he always would.

"I will take her back to the house." Ardal kept her close as he walked alongside the soldier.

"I can find my own way." Fiona shook his hand off her arm and pushed away.

She moved a few feet ahead of them. A burning sensation tickled her neck and she knew that both men watched her as she walked ahead. In the past it would have sent her into a panic attack. Now she didn't care. The sooner she was away from all men, the better.

The house felt cool after the hot glare of the sun. She went to the stove and turned the burner back on. Best to act like nothing important was happening. "Do your men require refreshments? Coffee or tea?"

"Nothing. We'll be finished soon." He left the house, closing the door behind him.

Ardal watched at the window for a few seconds and then turned to her. "Are you better?"

"Yes." Fiona heaved a sigh. "I usually don't cry. It was stupid to get upset. Why did you let them search?"

"It was safer." Ardal reached for the door handle. "I do not want them to think that we are hiding something."

"Well, we are." Fiona pushed her hair away from her face.

"If they get suspicious, I will kill them."

Fiona inhaled sharply. "Then the place will be crawling with soldiers."

Ardal nodded. "True. It would slow down our escape."

Nothing ruffled the man. "Where are Firbin and Jehon?"

"Following orders."

Fiona's eyes narrowed. "And the Captain?"

"Firbin took care of him."

"He didn't kill him?" Fiona's heart started beating rapidly. "I thought we'd agreed."

"He put him somewhere safe." Ardal opened the door. "I will be back once the soldiers have left."

"Fine." Fiona muttered a few choice words under her breath. It was just as well he didn't understand some of the more colorful words of the English language because she didn't feel like explaining them.

He waited until she'd stopped. "Is there something else you wish?"

"No, everything is wonderful." Fiona forced a mock smile onto her face.

"You lie. You have no reason to fear." Ardal hesitated a second before stepping closer to her. "I will not let these men harm you."

Fiona couldn't pull her eyes away from his. Sincerity shone from them. Never had she felt so safe before. "I know."

"I need to make sure these men leave." He turned and left the house.

Fiona sank into one of her kitchen chairs. Her hands were shaking. How could a man she barely knew affect her so deeply? It was insane. Yet she couldn't deny how she felt.

Ardal walked toward the barn and took a deep breath to steady his heart rate. So this was what it felt like to care for a woman. No wonder it was forbidden for Hunters. Never in all of his thirty-five years had Ardal experienced this before. His men's safety should be all that he was concerned with, but that was not what consumed his thoughts.

It was Fiona.

The ancient scripts said that Hunters were not from Cygnus. The Cygnusians had taken them from an inferior and primitive planet because they would make perfect warriors. Hunter genetics were considered inferior. The Cygnusians had improved them, but allowing a Hunter to mate made him useless. They became uncontrollable, refusing simple orders and worse, it was discovered that Hunters formed permanent attachments with their mates. They became unreliable and unfocused.

There was truth in this. Fiona haunted him. When the Captain had questioned her, his chest had tightened with anger. They were standard interrogation tactics. As a warrior he understood the need, but how dare the Captain harass her. He shook his head at his inconsistency, but seeing tears in Fiona's eyes was worse pain than any wound he had received in battle. For that he would have killed the man. The only thing that had stopped him was his years of training and command.

He had to take control of this situation fast. He looked to the barn where the soldiers were just leaving and then glanced at the helicopter in the field. There was still a man guarding it, but that would not have stopped Jehon from following his orders. Soon he would know what he was dealing with.

He walked toward the soldiers, keeping his eyes on the lead man. It was good that Fiona was safe. Now he could focus on dealing with the threat that these men presented. If they were suspicious, then he would kill them before they could reach the helicopter.

The Captain was relaxed when he reached him. He stopped and waited for Ardal. The other two soldiers were joking to each other as they walked by their commander toward the helicopter

"Did you find anything?" Ardal kept his voice pleasant.

"Not a thing." The soldier gave him a brief smile, his eyes assessing as they searched his face. "How long have you lived here?"

"A few weeks." Ardal glanced toward the house. "She needed protection, so I came."

The soldier nodded. "Let me guess, ex-military and now you're a bodyguard."

Ardal grunted. He was not sure what a bodyguard was, but it sounded like a protector. "How did you know?"

"You carry yourself as if you've had a military background; that and the scars." The man nodded at Ardal's exposed arms. "Knife wounds?"

"Yes." In truth, lasers had sliced his skin numerous times.

"Where did you see action?"

The soldier relaxed his hold on his rifle, almost as if waiting for a reaction. Ardal knew that only a man secure in his abilities would chance that. He also knew that only a desperate man would try and take away this man's weapon.

"Everywhere." Ardal watched the man lift an eyebrow. "I was in the forces for over twenty years."

The man grinned. "You must've joined up when you turned eighteen. I'm not sure guarding people will be easier."

"It is not much different from soldiering." Ardal started walking toward the helicopter. The man fell in step with him.

"Is she going to be all right?" He jerked his head toward the house.

Ardal clenched his jaw. "She is no longer safe here."

"I'm sorry about that, but you know how it is. Orders are orders."

Ardal stopped a few feet away from the helicopter. "Yes, I know."

He stood back and watched the men board the machine. He remained standing tall until the vehicle lifted off the ground. The machine flew toward the back field, staying a few feet from the ground. These men were very thorough.

Ardal crossed his arms and waited until the machine had swung back across the field and then headed past him. He turned and made certain that it left Fiona's property before walking to the barn.

Firbin and Jehon were there ahead of him. "Any problems?"

Jehon shook his head. "I managed to look inside the machine. It would have been easy to fly. It was quite rudimentary."

"What weapons do they have?"

"Primitive. They have guns that shoot bullets and missiles. No lasers, no interrupters, no disintegrators."

Ardal's eyes narrowed. "What about their searching capabilities?"

"They have thermal equipment and they can see at night."

Ardal nodded. "The men are scattered. That should not raise any suspicions. What about the Captain?"

"Still sleeping," Firbin voice was full of disgust. "I cannot believe that he must live."

"It is so ordered."

"True." Firbin glanced toward the house. "She should be safe to stay here now."

"She comes with us." Ardal almost winced at the harshness of his own voice. "She has more to fear than the search parties."

Jehon cleared his throat. "Will we not be in more danger if she accompanies us?"

"Perhaps, but I promised to protect her. A Hunter does not betray his word."

Ardal looked toward the house and sighed. He did not need to justify his actions to his men, but it would be best if they understood. He would not tell them that she had already found a place in his heart. They would never understand that their leader could forget his training and breeding to such a degree.

"She is hiding from a man who abuses her." Ardal's voice shook with the horror of his words. "We have made it unsafe for her. He may be able to track her to this place now."

Jehon frowned. "Men do not honor women here?"

Ardal shook his head. "It seems not. They do not live by the same code as we do."

"So women do not rule on this planet?" Firbin moved closer. "What kind of a place have we crashed on?"

"One that requires us to protect Fiona." Ardal's voice was firm. "I will not forget that I am a Hunter. I have vowed to follow the Sacred Code, no matter what the rules are on this planet."

"As we all have." Jehon's voice was firm. "None of us would dishonor our beliefs. We will protect Fiona also."

Ardal looked at Firbin who nodded his agreement. "Then we must disappear from this place. The soldiers will keep returning to this area until they find what they are seeking."

They walked to the house. Jehon and Firbin veered off to the truck while Ardal went to get Fiona. She had already packed, so there should be no problem leaving right away. He opened the door and she almost fell out in her rush to meet him.

Ardal took the bag from her hand. "The men are waiting in the truck."

"I can't go."

Chapter 8

"We leave now." Ardal's voice was low, but the cold look in his eyes sent shivers down Fiona's spine. The man could be menacing when he wanted to be.

Fiona shook her head and straightened her shoulders. "I've had a message from the group that is protecting me. They've told me not to leave."

"What message?"

"It was on my voicemail."

"You mail your voice?"

Fiona rolled her eyes. "It's like a recorder. When you don't pick up your phone people can still talk into it. They must have called when we were with the soldiers."

Fiona went back into the house. She had her orders and she wasn't budging from this place until someone from the group came to get her. She owed them too much to just ignore their advice.

"Why would they send this message?" Ardal left the door open behind him.

"I asked them for advice."

"What did you tell them?" Ardal turned her to face him.

Fiona shrugged off his hands. "I didn't mention you or your men. I just said that the military was looking around the area for someone."

"They do not have all the facts. It is not possible for them to make an informed decision." Ardal shook his head. "You will only be protected with us. We leave now."

"I have to stay. I promised." Fiona bit her lower lip. "You don't understand. If it wasn't for these people I wouldn't have survived this long. They know what they're doing. They've helped hundreds of other women."

"There are more women who need protection?" Ardal threw his head back and sighed. "What kind of world is this?"

"Not very good sometimes," Fiona whispered.

"Why would these people want you to live here on your own?"

"They think it's unlikely that David will hear about the possible crash. Even if he does, he won't connect it with me."

Ardal looked out the window, his brow furrowed in thought. Fiona held her breath as she waited for his decision. He was a man used to being obeyed. She had to be safe, though. That meant staying here.

Ardal turned with a swift movement. "No. We leave now."

A flicker of disappointment tugged at Fiona's heart. "I understand. You must leave the area before anyone discovers the truth."

"Yes, but you come with us."

"Look I panicked earlier. There's no possible way people will learn about the crash. If they do, it's not headline news."

"What about Marshall and Clyde? I do not trust those men. They looked at you with lust in their eyes."

Fiona gave a choked laugh. "They won't harm me."

"They will call other people to investigate." Ardal motioned around the house. "Then how secure will you be?"

Horror seeped through every nerve in her body. Television cameras and UFO fanatics would be swarming the place. She hugged her arms to her chest. Even if she refused to speak, they would be on the property. Nothing stopped fanatics. How soon would it be before her face was plastered on a tabloid with some outrageous comment below her name?

"I see you understand." Ardal took her arm and led her to the door. "These messages you send and receive, do they have to come from just one device?"

Fiona's mind went blank for a second; barely registering that she was outside the house. "Why do you want to know about telephones?"

"Can you leave a message from any telephone?" Ardal picked up her bag and started leading her to the truck.

"Of course. It doesn't matter where you call from, you'll reach the person you dialed."

"Then you can message these underground friends of yours from another place and they won't know the difference?"

Fiona let herself be helped into the truck. "You could tell I was calling from a different phone, but they'd get the message."

Ardal motioned to Jehon to start the vehicle. "So we can travel and still contact them."

"But will it be safe?"

"We have all vowed to protect you." Ardal's words were low.

Fiona shivered with the intensity of his look. The man wasn't kidding when he said it was a vow. She glanced at Jehon, who was driving, his hands tight on the wheel, his focus unwavering. Behind was Firbin, sprawled out on the extra seat of the extended cab. His arms were crossed but he looked at her with the same intensity as Ardal.

"Won't I hinder your escape?" Fiona wanted to accept their help, but a part of her knew that was selfish. These men, whether they were aliens or not, needed to find a refuge.

"Your life comes before ours."

Fiona felt tears start in her eyes. This was crazy. "No, it doesn't. You need to hide."

"So do you." Ardal brushed a tear from her cheek. "We are the same."

"I suppose." Fiona sniffed. "What if I hold you up?"

"We will wait." Ardal eased her back against the seat. "You need to sleep."

"I suppose I could explain things to you." Fiona covered her yawn with her hand. "Earth's people probably seem strange."

"You will be a help."

Fiona thought she caught a hint of sarcasm in Ardal's voice, but when she glanced up, he was looking at her with sincerity. Oh well, she didn't have much choice now. They were already on the road heading toward Wawa.

"I'd take the northern route if I were you." Sleep seemed to skirt around her senses. "They haven't found the other part of your vehicle so it's probably in Lake Superior. The further you get away from it, the better."

"Jehon has already considered that." Ardal rubbed her arm. "Sleep."

Fiona was too tired to argue. Her eyelids were heavy and before she could think of a response, she had drifted off. She woke with a start. Her head was cushioned against Ardal's chest. She sat up. The vehicle wasn't moving and Ardal was looking down at her expectantly.

"What?" Fiona stretched. They were stopped at the side of the road. She glanced out and saw a mileage sign for Chapleau in 10 kilometres. So they'd taken her advice and gone north.

"The vehicle is flashing a light at us." Jehon pointed to the dashboard.

Fiona leaned over his arm and spotted the low fuel sign. "We need gas."

"What do we do?" Ardal shifted beside her.

"We're almost at a town. There will be a gas station there."

Less than five minutes later they made the circular entry into the small town of Chapleau. Fiona spotted the gas station and motioned Jehon to drive to it. Once there, she pointed to the pumps.

"Pull up there and then turn the vehicle off." Fiona twisted around and spoke to Firbin. "Hand me my bag."

Fiona rummaged in her bag until her fingers touched the cloth pouch that contained her emergency kit. She had been taught to always take this with her, no matter how ridiculous it might seem. You never knew when you might have to make a run for it unexpectedly. Now was definitely one of those times. She opened the pouch and pulled out a wad of money.

"This is what you use to buy things."

"How do you get this?"

Fiona shrugged. "Usually people work and get paid money. Sometimes they save it in a bank and then they use an ATM machine to get the money."

"What is an ATM machine?"

Fiona pointed to one of the machines inside the convenience store doors. "You have a card that you put in to access your money. The machine will give you money from your bank account."

"We will let the others know."

Fiona frowned. "Do your scanners work as telephones?"

"The frequency is not right for that." Ardal opened the door and stepped out of the vehicle.

"I used to have a cell phone, but I had to get rid of it." Fiona jumped out of the truck and went to the pump. "They make it easy to stay in touch with people anywhere, but not if you're hiding. They all have GPS in them so that you can be found."

"This is an electronic device?" Ardal watched as she unscrewed the gas cap and then took the nozzle from the pump.

"Sort of." Fiona pushed the button on the pump and then started to fill the tank. "They have cell towers all around the country so that you can call from anywhere. The problem is that in remote areas like this, there are no towers."

"We will not need to use this way to communicate."

Fiona tilted her head. The man gave nothing away. She felt in her bones he was hiding something; some alien technology or way of communicating. But did it really matter?

"I can see you have no intention of telling me." Fiona shrugged.

"I have to protect my men."

The pump stopped. Fiona tapped the last drops of gas from the nozzle and then put it back into its slot before screwing the cap back on. "Come, I'll show you how to buy something. A word of warning; keep your head low. There are security cameras everywhere, especially in gas stations."

Ardal nodded his understanding and then followed her into the small store. She pulled out five twenty dollar bills and paid the attendant. After that she went to the back of the store where there were a number of tourist items, including tee shirts and hoodies. She pulled off a 2XL sized hoodie and held it up to Ardal.

"This'll fit." She then grabbed two other hoodies and three tee shirts. "You guys need to fit in. These should help."

They walked back to the front and Fiona noticed that Ardal kept in front of her the whole time. There was no way the security cameras would be able to see her behind his huge body. She paid and as she waited for her change, she glanced down.

Her eyes roamed the rows of candy and chips. She was a sucker for junk food, especially when she was stressed. Her hands hovered between a chocolate bar and a pack of chewing gum. Chocolate won out. She glanced at Ardal who seemed fascinated by her choice.

"What is that?"

"Chocolate. It's sweet, decadent, and definitely not good for you." Fiona smiled and picked up four of the bars. "We deserve this."

Once they were back in the truck, Fiona handed out the clothes. "Put these on. When you have to go outside it would be best to put the hood up over your heads. That should make it difficult for the security cameras to pick out your faces."

"Are there lots of these cameras?" Ardal pulled the hoodie on, stretching it over his bulging muscles.

"More than you'd think. If it isn't store owners, it's the government." Fiona winced as she remembered her first attempts to escape David.

"I will warn the others."

Fiona nodded. "The government or even a person who is internet savvy can tap into any of these systems and find people they're looking for."

The others were now in their new sweatshirts and Fiona nodded her approval before handing out the chocolate bars. The men hesitated and watched Fiona rip open the wrapping and take a bite. Gooey caramel dripped down her chin. She wiped it away with a finger. She leaned back and closed her eyes. After the day she'd had, this was heaven.

Jehon was the first to try it. "It is too sweet to eat."

"That's the point." Fiona grinned. "Nothing about this is good for you, but isn't it fun?"

"Will we be ill?" Firbin piped up from the back.

"Not unless you're allergic to chocolate." Fiona looked back at him and watched as his eyes widened after his first bite. "Addictive isn't it?"

Ardal sat beside her with his eyes closed and arms crossed. She was going to nudge him, but Jehon stopped her. He shook his head and she realized that somehow he was communicating with the others. She went back to her chocolate bar.

Jehon started the truck. When Ardal relaxed beside her, she offered him his chocolate bar, but he shook his head. His jaw was still clenched and his eyes were furrowed in a frown. Definitely time to give the man some space.

Fiona dozed throughout the trip. Jehon seemed tireless. He drove nonstop without a break. Her stomach started growling in the early evening and her bladder was screaming. The men seemed unaware of her discomfort.

"Are we stopping soon?" She tried to keep the irritation out of her voice.

"Why would we stop?" Ardal looked down at her with a frown. "Jehon thinks we might be able to reach the city by morning."

"Don't you guys ever have to relieve yourselves?"

"Relief from what?"

"Not relief, relieve, as in empty your bladder?" She almost screamed when she caught Ardal's look of confusion. "I need to go to the washroom."

"You wish to wash yourself?" Ardal's eyes widened. "Of course, the chocolate bar has made you dirty. Jehon has a cloth for you."

"I have to pee." Fiona groaned. She wanted to hide her face from the embarrassment. Talking about this with a bunch of men was bad enough, but to have them totally misunderstand was beyond the limit. Ardal still looked dumbfounded.

"When you drink water on your planet how does your body get rid of it?"

Comprehension suddenly dawned on Ardal. His face turned a ruddy red and he lowered his eyes. "Hunters do not discuss such matters."

"I'm trying not to discuss it." Fiona glanced out the window. "There's a restaurant over there. Stop."

Jehon slammed on the brakes so fast that Fiona would have gone through the windshield if Ardal hadn't put out his arm to stop her. These guys had phenomenal reflexes. Fiona rubbed her sides. At least her ribs were still intact.

Jehon pulled into the parking lot and then turned to her. "What do you want?"

Fiona rolled her eyes. It was obvious that she was going to have to explain everything to them. "I want to use the washroom and then get something to eat. You might be able to go without food for days, but my stomach is protesting."

"Your stomach has been talking to all of us." Ardal's tone was dry, his face impassive, but there was a sparkle in his eyes.

"You just made a joke." Fiona laughed. "And I thought you didn't hear it growling."

"That is an apt name for what it was doing." Ardal pulled his hood over his head before leaving the vehicle. "It seems we are hypersensitive on this planet."

"Good." Fiona scooted along the truck's bench seat and then jumped down. "Next time you'll know what it means and stop before I go through the windshield."

Firbin squeezed from the back and eased himself outside. "A Hunter never fails in his protection. You were safe."

"Tell my ribs that." Fiona rubbed the still sensitive muscles. "You don't know your strength, or else it's another thing that earth has made extraordinary."

Ardal shrugged. "Perhaps. We will test it later."

Jehon came around the vehicle and looked at the front of the truck stop diner. "Is this a good place to stop?"

"No worse than most. I'm glad you're with me, though. This is trucker territory and I hate having to walk into a place like this on my own."

Fiona started toward the restaurant. Truckers were usually men. They were polite and kept to themselves, but even though she had stopped at places like this before, she was never alone. There was safety in numbers.

When she got closer to the entrance she noticed a number of motorcycles parked together. Great! This must be a local hangout. It was worse when she opened the door. Everybody and their brother had decided to stop and eat. The place was packed. She pushed back the panic she felt at having to face such a large number of men at once.

"It must be a good place to eat." She kept her voice steady as she looked around for the washroom sign. She was rewarded immediately. "You guys can either go and find an empty table, or wait for me here."

"It might be best to find a place to sit." Ardal glanced around the crowded dining area. "Is this how people eat here?"

"Only when they're travelling." Fiona kept her voice low. "Truckers are travelling all the time because they're carrying goods in their vehicles and they have to get from one place to another. There are also people like us here."

"They are hiding?" Jehon's voice was doubtful.

"I meant they're hungry." Fiona moved toward the washroom. "Just behave until I get back."

The restroom was clean. That was the best thing she could say about it. It was a relief to be alone. As much as she liked people, it had been months since she'd been around others. Her enforced isolation had made her more self-reliant. She refused to consider she'd also been lonely and bored. She'd been safe. That was all that mattered.

Ardal and his men weren't in sight when she came out of the restroom. They must have sat at a table so she made her way into the dining room. It was a sea of faces and it took her a while to find the men. They were in a back corner booth glancing at menus. She wondered if they could read.

A smile flickered across her lips. What a terrible thing to think. If she were in a foreign country, not even a different planet, she'd be totally lost.

"Are you looking for company, little lady?" A man in full leather jacket and pants was standing in front of her. A band of orange was engraved on the leather of his sleeve and the strong odor of cigarette smoke clung to him.

"I'm meeting friends." Fiona tried to go around him, but he sidestepped to block her.

"I was asking politely."

"And I answered you politely." Fiona inhaled to settle her rapid heart rate. "My friends are in the corner."

The man looked over his shoulder. "Hear that boys? This lady doesn't want to spend time with us." The biker turned back to her. "You'll be sitting with me, and you'll like it, sweet thing."

Chapter 9

A man with a full beard and baseball cap turned and spoke from the nearest table. "The lady said no."

"Stay out of this, Grandpa." The biker didn't take his eyes off Fiona. "I'd hate to see you regret your words."

"If that's what it takes to make you boys understand." The man stood up and a couple of his neighbours joined him.

Horror raced through Fiona's body. She didn't want a war between these bikers and truckers. "Please," she pleaded. "I just want to go and eat."

"Then you'll have no problem doing it with me." The biker's voice was a threat.

Just as the older trucker and his friends moved to block the man in leather, someone grabbed him from behind and lifted him off the floor. She had barely registered that Ardal had come to her rescue before the man was sent flying against the wall. His body slithered to the floor. His face was red with anger as he jumped up and came back at Ardal full speed.

Ardal blocked him with one hand and sent him flying again. "Stay."

For a second it looked as if the biker was going to refuse, but then his mouth thinned and he nodded. "I'll see to you later."

Ardal's eyes hardened. "It would be a mistake."

The trucker cleared his throat. "Nice throw, young man. Glad to see the little lady has some protection. It doesn't do for one so pretty to be alone."

Fiona gave the man a faint smile. "Thank you for trying to stop it from getting out of control."

"No problem." The man nodded to the waiter standing a few feet away. "Anything serious happens and old John there would have called the cops."

"I'm glad that wasn't necessary." Fiona forced her voice to relax. "I'm too hungry to wait for the police."

Ardal moved to let her pass. She started to walk, but realized that he'd stayed behind to talk to the trucker. When she got to the table, Jehon and Firbin stood and waited until she was seated before sitting themselves. Ardal followed a few minutes later.

"What did the trucker say?"

"He warned me that the fellow I threw would probably kill me." Ardal grunted. "I thanked him, but said I had many years of training. He said he guessed I was probably in the Special Forces. It seems he spent some time there and would be happy to help me if I needed it."

"What did you say?" Fiona forced her jaw closed.

"I said that I had friends with me." Ardal picked up the menu. "What are Special Forces?"

"I suppose it's our planet's equivalent of an elite soldier." Fiona studied Ardal's face for a second, noting his strong jaw and straight nose. An air of confidence and command surrounded him. No wonder the older man had associated him with a Special Forces background.

Ardal nodded. "The man was very observant."

"I think they're trained to be." Fiona sighed and picked up her menu. "Thank you for saving me."

"I thought you did not want trouble. I see the rule does not apply to you."

Fiona opened her mouth to defend herself when she noticed the sparkle in Ardal's eyes. "You're joking again." She pushed against his arm. "I thought you didn't understand sarcasm."

"It is fun to make you blush."

Before Fiona could say anything, the waiter was at their table. He brought four glasses of water and then stood back with his pad, ready for their orders. She grabbed the menu and made a decision for the broasted chicken. Chocolate and now fried food. Her diet was going for a tumble, but what the hell. At the rate that she was going, she might not live to see the end of the week, much less old age.

When the waiter looked at Ardal, she noticed a tightening in his jaw. She was right, they couldn't read. She grabbed the menu from him. "Let me guess, you'd like a steak." She glanced at Jehon and Firbin across the table. "You guys want that also?"

When they nodded the waiter took the order and then headed off to the next table. Once he was out of earshot, she leaned forward. "Did you guys understand the menu?"

"No." Ardal clenched his fists. "The translator download was incomplete. What is steak?"

"It's beef and tastes a bit like the moose you guys killed." Fiona took a sip of water. "This is water. I imagine you have this on your planet."

Ardal drank his down without a stop. "It is different in taste. We only have artificial water."

"Don't you have natural sources of it?"

Ardal shook his head. "Not on Cygnus."

"How do you survive?" Fiona couldn't keep the surprise out of her voice. "What happened to it?"

"The ancients were careless." Ardal shrugged. "We make it, or import it from other planets."

Fiona picked up her fork and started to fiddle with it. "You should tell me what things are different from what you're used to."

"That is probably everything, although Jehon was able to ascertain what equipment the helicopter had for tracking us." Ardal took the fork from her. "What is this for?"

"Eating." Fiona grabbed it back and demonstrated. "I'm sure you know what a knife is." When Ardal nodded, she picked up the spoon. "You stir with this or eat, but usually only soup or cereal."

"We have similar on our planet." Ardal leaned back against the bench seat and looked at Jehon. "How long do you need to repair the communicators?"

Jehon shook his head. "Each one has different damage. It is most important that your unit work, though. I will look at it now."

Ardal handed over the device that looked like a miniature tablet. Jehon leaned over the object, using his one arm to hide it from others. Within seconds his fingers were dancing around the screen followed by a blur of color and noises.

"Jehon is an expert with machines." Ardal's voice was low. "He will not make a mistake."

Fiona sighed. She was way too tense. Too much had happened in the last twelve hours, never mind spending the last year of her life in hiding. Worrying was wasted energy. Energy she'd need later if today was any indication.

"How do your people read?" Fiona leaned her head back. "Do you use letters like we do?"

"Our language is a combination of symbols and images. It was given to us by the ancients."

"Who are the ancients?" Fiona traced her finger around a water ring on the table.

Ardal watched the light play across Fiona's features. She was truly beautiful. It had been a mistake to bring her into a place with so many men. There was the odd woman eating, but they paled in comparison to Fiona. Beauty such as hers would make men forget themselves, especially on a planet that had no rules to control men.

She was a brave woman. Despite the fright she must have had from the man at the entrance, she was now trying to relax. Questions about his home land would take her mind off the problems they were facing. Despite being quite a distance from the farm, he knew that it was only a matter of time before the military noticed that they'd left. Then the search would begin again.

"The ancients were a group of men and women who set out the rules for our people." Ardal kept his voice low. "They decided that women were the most suited to rule and that men should be their mates."

"So you have left your mates on your home planet." Fiona turned around and looked at him, her eyes glistening with unshed tears. "Do you have any children?"

Firbin moved forward as if to speak, but Ardal lifted his hand. He would explain all to Fiona. It was his right as leader and also his desire. He was connected to her in a way that had never happened to him before. She must know that even though he was attracted to her, he would not take advantage of that.

"Hunters are not permitted to mate."

"Never?" Fiona glanced at the other men at the table. "None of you have a wife or children?"

"No."

Fiona frowned and then shook her head. "How do you get new Hunters?"

"We were bred in birthing chambers. Our genes were chosen so that we would be the best possible Hunters." Ardal's jaw tightened as flashes of his early life bombarded him. "Then we were raised to fight."

"You had no childhood?" Fiona's words were a whisper.

"It was necessary to make great Hunters."

"Why can't you have a wife or children?" Fiona's frowned. "That has nothing to do with being a Hunter."

"We do not have such things on our planet."

"Nobody does?"

"The Kaladin choose mates as they desire, but they are not permanent. A Hunter was forbidden to mate." Ardal watched horror, revulsion, and then sadness play across Fiona's face. She hid nothing. "How do you do it on earth?"

Her eyes softened. "Two people fall in love and then marry. If they wish, they have children and raise them. They form a family."

"So you have this?"

"No." Her chest heaved on a sigh. "Some people mistake power and possession for love. They think that they own the other person and will do everything possible to keep that person."

"This David thinks he owns you."

Fiona shook her head. "He's sick. We dated a couple of times. It was enough for me." Fiona raised her hand to push her hair off her face. "I didn't want to go out with him, but he insisted on dinner.

"You mated after this meal?" Firbin leaned closer to Fiona, his eyes wide with interest.

Ardal struggled to control the surge of anger that flowed through his body. The thought of Fiona with this faceless David was enough to make him want to kill. He clenched his fists and fought the urge to pound them through the table.

"What kind of girl do you think I am?" Fiona's indignation and anger broke through Ardal's thoughts.

"What did I say wrong?" Firbin frowned.

"You think I have sex with every man I meet?"

Fiona's voice was loud enough for the people in the next table to glance over. Ardal forced a smile and then reached for her hand. He touched her, unprepared for the sizzle of intensity that shot through his arm. Fiona seemed to feel it also because her eyes widened and she looked down at their joined hands.

"We are trying to understand how your world works." Ardal kept his voice low, stating each word slowly. "On Cygnus, women mate frequently with men they just meet."

"I'm sorry." Fiona's hand fluttered beneath his. "I'm causing a scene, but whenever I think of him, my body crawls with disgust. I didn't encourage him, but he wouldn't leave me alone. When I said no, he forced himself."

Firbin gasped and Jehon looked up from the communicator. Ardal squeezed Fiona's hand. He had never come across this before. Men on his planet lived to please their women, not harm them. That was one of the reasons Hunters could not mate. Their training and genetics meant that the Ancients feared that they would not be able control their emotions.

Firbin was the first to speak. "He hurt you?"

Fiona nodded and then looked down. "He's insane."

"We have sworn to protect you." Jehon spoke with force. "There is no need to worry."

"Knowing that you're safe and feeling safe aren't the same thing." Fiona gave a Jehon a crooked smile.

With sudden insight, Ardal understood. She was like a wounded animal seeking shelter. A man had done this to her, so only a man could fix it. No matter how frustrating or irrational her demands, he must ensure that they were followed. Showing that he and his men would not hurt her was the first step to getting her to trust them.

Just then the waiter brought them their meals. Ardal looked down at the steak that she had ordered and picked up his fork and knife. The first bite told him that she had chosen well. He was used to going without food for days at a time, but it was best to take advantage of this opportunity. Fiona had been right to stop.

"Your food is good."

Ardal watched as Firbin ate with the enthusiasm of the young. Had he ever eaten without a care? Probably, in the days before leadership and responsibility had taken their toll. Now he could only focus on how to get his men and Fiona to a safe place. Fiona required watching. Just walking into the diner had created a situation.

He had reacted without considering the consequences. This was not part of his training, but he did not regret his actions. A Hunter kept his word and never retreated. This world had strange rules, ones that caused harm to the innocent and favored the strong. But was that different from Cygnus?

Centuries of harmony meant Kaladin rule had never been questioned. The use of warriors was restricted to other planets. Hunters were seldom allowed on Cygnus. The Kaladin did not want to be reminded that violence was used to protect them. They considered themselves a peaceful people.

He had come to terms with this when he was a young man. He did not think less of the people who gave the orders. It was not his place to judge, only to obey. Now there were no orders to follow. He must assess this world and make the decisions that would give his men honor and still let them live as they had been bred.

"Do you want dessert?" Fiona leaned back and patted her stomach. "I'm full, but I never pass up the opportunity of dessert."

Ardal smiled. It looked as if Fiona had forgotten her earlier upset. "What is dessert?"

"Well, it could be healthy like fruit, or bad like chocolate."

"Chocolate." Firbin enthused.

Fiona leaned forward and motioned to the waiter. "Four chocolate cheesecakes and coffees. We'll have a little bad with good."

The first bite of cheesecake was a surprise. It was a velvety smoothness that held a bit of tartness with the sweet of chocolate. Fiona was right. It was a bit of bad and a bit of good. Perhaps that was how life on this planet was going to be. He never thought about good or bad, only doing his duty.

"Who else will be chasing us?" The words were out before he could stop them.

Fiona swallowed and pointed her fork at him. "Just about everybody."

"Could you narrow that?"

"Well, the military you already know about. We're lucky if we get away from law enforcement, but somehow I think the way you tossed that biker is on a security camera somewhere. Who knows where that will show up? Probably on the Internet."

"Explain Internet."

"That's where the computers can access all kinds of information. People, places, pictures, and words and then others can look at it." Fiona took another bite and closed her eyes.

"How do we close down this Internet?"

Fiona choked. She coughed for several seconds before taking a sip of water. "You can't shut down the internet. Too many people and businesses all over the world use it."

"So what you can't defeat, you use." This was one of the rules of the Warrior Code. There was wisdom in the code. Even in this strange land it would help him make decisions. "How do we use the Internet?"

"You can start with a website, but you'd have to have something to put on it."

"Can we ensure that others do not use it to find us?"

Fiona shrugged. "No. The best thing is to keep a low profile." Fiona took another bite of her desert. "I'll tell you one thing though, once the ufologists get wind of the crash, they're going to be crawling around looking for evidence of aliens."

Ardal took a deep breath. Would this world ever make any sense? "What is a ufologist?"

"People who hunt UFOs."

"And that is?" Ardal prodded.

"It's an unidentified flying object." Fiona shrugged. "Extra-terrestrials or aliens. They're obsessed with them. They have magazines, television shows, and tons of stuff about them on the Internet."

So people on this planet searched for people from other planets. "How many aliens have landed here?"

Fiona took her last bite and then pulled the cup with dark liquid toward her. She poured in white liquid, pursed her lips, and took a sip. She sighed and put the cup back on the table before looking at him.

"Most sane people don't believe aliens exist."

"So there are none?"

"I'm not so sure now." Fiona bit her lip. "I think the people who believe in them might be saner than the rest of us."

"So we must find these others. They may help us." Firbin leaned forward on the table.

"They may harm us." Jehon's gaze did not leave Ardal.

They had been through many battles together and he trusted Jehon's instinct. His own gut told him that it might be dangerous to try and find others. Who knew where they were from? They might be enemies, or they might be searchers looking for Hunters.

"Jehon is right." Ardal took a sip of the dark liquid. Heat burned its way down his throat. "To keep your enemy unaware is the best defense."

"We keep a low profile." Ardal gave his men a steady look. There was no further need to elaborate. They understood and would obey.

He took another sip of his drink. "What is this?"

"Coffee." Fiona grinned. "It has caffeine in it. It sort of speeds the body up and keeps you awake."

"An enhancer?"

Fiona frowned. "That's one way of putting it. What's an enhancer?"

"Chemicals or devices used to improve our performance."

"Drugs?" Fiona's voice held a note of shock.

Ardal shrugged. Enhancers were a part of his life. Whether he ingested them or they were implanted. A Hunter used whatever means necessary to achieve his goal. He did not fail.

"We use what helps us succeed."

"That sounds so cold-blooded." Fiona shivered and then took another sip of coffee. "The worst thing that coffee will do is keep you awake at night."

"Then it has a use." Ardal finished his cup. "Let us leave."

They gathered their stuff and stood. Out of the corner of his eye he noticed the bikers scramble out of the restaurant. That could only mean trouble. He made a move to follow them outside, but Fiona put her hand on his arm.

She handed him money. "Sometimes it looks better if the man pays."

Ardal felt a tightening in his chest. In the past women relied on him to protect them and to obey. Never had he been asked to step forward and take on a woman's role. He glanced at Jehon and Firbin, who were both frowning. This planet was upside down, but it was going to be their home. He had better get used to it.

Ardal nodded at the old trucker who had tried to defend Fiona. "Glad to see you have a couple of friends," the man said in a gruff voice. "My name's George, by the way. Remember my warning."

"We will be fine." Ardal paid the bill. He looked outside, but the bikes were all gone. He opened the door for Fiona to pass before him.

George followed them outside. "I should warn you. Those boys are a mean bunch."

"We will guard for them."

"I'm sure you will, but those bikers are members of the FD Warriors, one of the worse outlaw gangs in North American." The trucker paused and looked behind him before continuing. "They're nothing but a problem, what with their violence and drug running. They think they own the roads and trust me, we truckers have a better handle on it than they do."

Fiona rubbed her arms. "We don't want trouble."

"You've got it whether you want it or not." George walked with them to their truck. "Those boys can't let it be known that you bested them in public. They'll come for you."

"There must be people who aren't afraid of them?" Fiona's voice wavered. "You stood up against them."

"That's because I've seen enough of their bullying to make me sick." George leaned in close, his voice low. "The last young girl they accosted ended up dead. She was no more than eighteen and her body was mutilated almost beyond recognition. I vowed then that I wouldn't sit by and let them get away with it again."

There was only one option. "We will kill them then." Ardal's voice was firm.

"You can't kill everybody who gets in your way. The police will be after us." Fiona's voice was a low whisper.

"They will hunt us later." Ardal gave her a steady stare. "One such as that does not know reason."

George nodded. "Then plan it. Make sure you're somewhere remote enough that the bodies will never be found and you don't have witnesses. That way the authorities won't have cause to put you in prison."

This was a strange world indeed.

On one hand there was violence that he usually only saw during war, and on the other, a concern for the pretense of law and order.

"So we should ambush them and cover evidence of it."

The trucker raised an eyebrow and nodded. "Bingo."

"What about the police?" Fiona shivered in the cool night air. "Can't they help?"

George shook his head. "They try, but the FDs always seem to be a couple of steps ahead. I'd hate to think what they'd do to a pretty young lady like you."

Ardal clenched his fists. Women and children were not safe when men went around hurting and threatening them. The men on this planet were breaking the most sacred of the codes that he was sworn to defend. He could not stand by and do nothing.

"How can people live like this?"

"You're not from around here." George put his hand up when Ardal opened his mouth to answer. "I don't want to know. I've seen too many strange things driving these roads at night. All I can say is that despite good intentions, you'll always find those who choose evil."

Ardal nodded. There were many people who lived selfish lives. The Holman were a good example of that. Power and control was what they desired and they did not care how they achieved it. He and his men were in a strange land, but this was their home now. They would have to choose how they lived in it.

"Now if I were you gentlemen, I'd get into my truck and get out of here before the police show up." The man nodded back toward the diner. "You've done nothing wrong, but seeing how those bikers tore out of here, you can be certain someone in there called them."

"We will leave." Ardal opened the door of the truck and waited for Fiona to jump in.

"Good luck boys." George held out his hand and waited for Ardal to grab it. He shook his hand and then released it. "You keep safe. That pretty young lady needs you alive and free."

Once the truck had pulled away, he turned to Fiona. "The man touched and shook my hand. Why?"

"That's how people greet each other, or say goodbye, or agree to something." Fiona sighed and relaxed against the seat. "Remind me not to take you guys out to dinner again."

Ardal leaned against the door and considered the trucker's advice. To follow the Sacred Code and live with honor, he must learn to be secretive. It would not be difficult because a Hunter usually tracked and killed in secret. What was different was hiding his actions from the authorities.

Fiona was quiet, but her hands were clenched and tight on her lap. Ardal put his hand over hers and squeezed. "We will not allow any harm to come to you."

"You can't promise that." Fiona inhaled sharply. "These gang members are ruthless, evil men. They are criminals who take and do what they want."

"We are Hunters." Ardal leaned close to her. "I will defend you with my last breath."

Fiona looked up at him, her eyes pleading. "Would you promise to kill me if necessary?"

Ardal understood her fear. She would rather die than let these men harm her. She did not yet understand the skill of a Hunter. "It will not come to that, but if it eases your mind, I will promise."

"Thank you," Fiona said in a shaky voice.

Ardal suppressed the sudden urge to pull her close and kiss her. He inhaled a steadying breath and released her hands. This attraction was insanity. Never had he felt the smallest inclination to be close to a woman before.

Before he could consider how to distance himself from Fiona, the truck lights outlined several vehicles in the center of the highway. Jehon slammed on the brakes and they came to a skidding stop. All senses were alerted to trouble before he saw the first of the leather-clad bikers.

They had been ambushed.

Chapter 10

"Let us handle this." Ardal's voice seemed loud to her ears.

"There's too many."

Fiona couldn't think past the number of gang members who were blocking the highway. There had to be thirty or more. There was no way that Ardal and his men could defeat them.

"A Hunter has many talents."

Fiona's eye widened as Jehon stomped on the accelerator. He revved the engine of the truck until it sounded like a hurricane and then he released the brake. The vehicle went skidding and spinning toward the bikes on the road.

There was no mercy in his attack.

He sent five bikers flying across the front of their vehicle. Their bodies hit hard. The echo of the men crashing against the truck's metal reverberated in Fiona's ears even as she felt their bodies slamming against the road. The ones that were wearing helmets might live, but not the others.

Jehon broke through the barricade.

He spun the truck around.

Before the gang could react, he turned into a side road. He drove for several hundred feet and cranked the wheel so they faced the highway and then stopped. Ardal reached for a weapon from Firbin and opened the door.

"Stay."

He spat his order even as he leveled his gun at the first of the bikers roaring into the enclosed space. Firbin threw a weapon at Jehon and jumped the seat to follow Ardal.

Jehon grabbed his firearm and started out the door. "You will be safe," he said before leaving the truck.

How was that possible? In just a few seconds she'd seen more violence than she'd watched at the movies. To be fair, she only watched romantic comedies, but still, this was real life. These men were ruthless.

The FD Warriors had regrouped and were racing toward Ardal. He stood in the middle of the lane, his weapon extended. He didn't wait for the bikes to stop. He shot as they approached. His aim was deadly. One after another slumped on their machine and skidded off the road.

He walked straight into the moving bikes, Firbin and Jehon bringing up each side. They were merciless in their precision. They had killed about twenty more of the bikers before the pile of bodies and machines prevented the others from rushing them. The remaining FDs got off their bikes and walked through their fallen comrades toward the Hunters.

Ardal flexed his neck from side to side and stood with his legs apart, arms crossed over his chest, weapon in hand. His men were about ten feet away on either side, their stance mirroring their leader. They waited in silence until the remaining eight FDs stood in front of them.

"Impressive." The biker who'd accosted Fiona in the diner, kicked the bike of one of his fallen comrades. He pointed a gun at Ardal's chest "We're still going to kill you and take that sweet morsel of a female for our own."

"Walk away." Ardal's voice was a low growl.

He laughed. "You must be crazy."

"No, we are Hunters true and right." Ardal nodded to Jehon and Firbin.

The leader laughed and then took a few steps back so that his men could move forward. "Kill them," he yelled.

Before the man in front of Ardal could pull his trigger, Ardal had grabbed his arm and wrenched it up and then backwards with a bone crunching snap. The man screamed his agony just as Ardal shot him twice in the heart and silenced him.

The next Warrior rushed Ardal with a knife. He dodged the attack and then captured his opponent's hand and twisted it behind his back. A second later the knife was sticking out of the biker's back as he fell on the pile of dead.

The last man shot his gun at Ardal, but missed. The bullet hit the truck and Fiona couldn't stop her scream. Ardal looked back at her, his eyes narrowed, jaw clenched, before turning and killing the man with a shot to the forehead.

Firbin and Jehon killed their opponents as easily as Ardal. All that remained was the leader. His eyes widened and he shook his head at his fallen comrades. He raised his gun with a shaky hand and then stumbled backwards. He ran to the highway where a tractor trailer truck had screeched to a stop near the bikes on the road.

"He is mine." Ardal threw back at Firbin and Jehon. "Gather the dead."

Fiona scrambled out of the truck. She couldn't stay there a second longer. The horror of the deaths was bad enough, but the thought that Ardal would leave her alone, she couldn't handle. Even dead, these monsters terrified her. She had to be with Ardal.

She had to feel safe.

Fiona caught up to Ardal at the highway.

The lights from the semi illuminated the scene. Ardal was at the far side of the truck where the door was wide open. The leader of the FD Warriors was nowhere in sight. Neither was the driver of the transport. Fiona skidded to a stop. Her chest hurt and she bent to catch her breath.

Cold metal pressed against the side of her head.

Then her body was jerked upward.

Rough arms encased her and pulled her close. She was forced to the truck. "Now who wins?" Fiona shivered with revulsion as the biker's breath skimmed her ear.

Ardal stepped from behind the side of the semi. The old trucker, George, was with him. The two men advanced a few steps until they were in front of the biker. Fiona forced herself to breath. She needed to be ready for whatever happened.

"Only a coward stands behind a woman." Ardal's voice was scornful.

"Who cares? I get to leave."

"She will not protect you." Ardal wiped his bloody hands on his thighs.

"You're crazy, man." The biker pulled her closer and waved his gun in Ardal's direction.

Ardal didn't hesitate.

He grabbed the hand holding the pistol and twisted it back until Fiona heard the cracking of bones. Then he plucked the weapon from the biker's limp wrist. The man screamed his pain. Ardal's jaw tensed as he yanked him away from her. She stumbled backward and was caught by George.

Ardal picked the man up with one hand clasped around his throat and squeezed. The biker clawed at his hand; his frantic attempt to get loose useless. Ardal didn't release him. The Warrior's face turned blue and his eyes bulged as the life slowly ebbed from him.

Fiona shut her eyes and put her hands to her ears to block out the sound of the man's last breaths. She turned away, closing her eyes to the horror, but knowing it would never leave her. She'd replay the violence she'd seen for the rest of her life. She understood the need to kill the man, but that didn't make it any easier to deal with.

Ardal threw the man's body to the ground.

He turned to Fiona. "It is done."

Fiona shook free of George and ran to him. Her hands fluttered over his arms and chest, as she checked for wounds. There were none. The blood was from the bikers. With a sigh of relief, she put her forehead on his chest.

"You're not hurt."

"Hunters do not fall easily."

Ardal soothed her back with his hand, sending warmth through her body. It eased the coldness that the violence had left inside her. No matter how much she'd abhorred what had happened here, he'd been protecting her. She'd been stupid and allowed herself to be caught.

"It's my fault that he's dead." Her words were little more than a whisper, but he looked down at her.

"He threatened you. He was a coward and cruel." Ardal tilted her chin so that she could look into his eyes. "He gave me no choice. He caused his own death."

"If I'd stayed in the truck, he wouldn't have caught me."

"I would still have hunted him until I killed him." Ardal's voice was emotionless. "I could not allow him to live."

"I don't usually agree with killing, little lady, but that man wouldn't have stopped." George cleared his throat. "The world is a better place without him."

Fiona wished she believed that in her heart. Logically she knew they were right. There'd been no choice. It was either kill or be killed. Why did everything have to be so complicated, though? Life would be easier if there was only right and wrong.

Ardal cleared his throat and eased away from her. "The man had no honor."

He pulled the biker's body off the highway. He also pushed the fallen bikes to the edge. When the highway was cleared George returned to his truck. Ardal and Fiona followed him.

"I wouldn't stick around too long," he said as he climbed up to the cab of his vehicle. "I came to warn you that a couple of people were talking about calling the police out. They were afraid about what the FD Warriors would do."

"We leave immediately."

"You take care of that young lady." George's voice was gruff.

"Always."

"I've never seen the likes of a fighter like you. That might get you into trouble one of these days." George held out his hand. "If you ever need anything, just ask for old George at any of the stops along this run. I've been doing it for years."

"I will." Ardal shook his hand and watched as the semi moved onto the highway.

When the taillights had disappeared, Jehon and Firbin joined them. They all helped move the dead bodies and motorcycles to the side road and down to their truck where there was already a pile of bodies.

"Light it." Ardal's voice broke the silence.

Fiona glanced over her shoulder and saw the bodies set on fire. All evidence would be gone, but would she forget? The men didn't seem to have the same concerns. They stood with arms crossed and watched the flames consume the bodies.

It was over in a matter of minutes.

The bikes were also put together and Firbin pulled a bottle of fluid from the box of the truck and spilled it over the metal. He threw a match on it and it sparked into flames. It burned with a bright white light that sizzled and spit until it extinguished itself along with evidence of the bikes.

Daylight and closer scrutiny might show traces of melted metal, but someone would have to know where to look. This was probably how they'd disposed of the debris of their crash.

Ardal gave a final inspection of the site and then nodded to Jehon. Firbin climbed into the back and Jehon started the vehicle. Ardal waited for Fiona to sit down before squeezing in beside her.

They had only been driving a couple of minutes before the flashing lights of a patrol car shone through the windshield.

"It's the police." Fiona's heart started pounding.

"What will they do to us?" Ardal kept his eyes focused on the vehicle moving toward them.

"Nothing if we keep moving." Fiona bit her lip. "We broke all the rules. I should have known better than to stop and eat."

"You were hungry." Ardal gave her a brief smile. "We are the ones who made trouble."

"That's sweet of you to take the blame, but it was the Warriors." Fiona sighed. "If it wasn't for me though, they wouldn't have done anything."

The vehicle with flashing lights sped past them. Fiona turned around and watched it disappear in the night. There had to be something that could be done. To just sit and wait for the police to catch them seemed wrong. After all, they were the victims here.

"You guys are supposed to be hunters on your planet, right?" She couldn't believe she was going to ask this. "What do you do when you're chased?"

"Hide."

"Well I know that." Fiona let out an exasperated breath. "How would you do it in this situation and would it be legal?"

"Anything a Hunter does is legal." Ardal straightened his shoulders. "A Hunter only acts when someone has broken the codes, or under the orders of the Kaladin."

"So no one questions what you do?" Well that explained the devil may care attitude toward killing someone. If no one came after them they could do whatever they wanted. "Do you ever have a situation that isn't so easy?"

"Frequently." Ardal gave her a hard stare. "Hunters are used when things go wrong. We make situations right. We make things disappear."

"Really?" Fiona's voice sounded like a squeak. These guys sounded like CIA Black Ops or something. "How does something disappear?"

"You erase all traces of it." Ardal's voice sounded bored. "It is what we are trained for. We hunt what is lost or hidden, and we make what is a problem disappear. The disappearance of the bikers was not one of our best efforts."

"They took us by surprise."

"That is not the reason." Ardal spoke without emotion. "We were rushed and being chased by the authorities. Our disposal of the bikes was sloppy. On Cygnus our carelessness would not have been tolerated."

Fiona's heart was starting to beat rapidly. Just who the hell had crashed on her property? These guys sounded like someone's worse nightmare. And yet they had protected her. They seemed to have a code they followed and rules were important to them.

Their rules didn't mesh with the laws on earth, though.

It would only take the police a short time to figure out they'd passed them or the FD Warriors on their way to the diner. Soon there would be a lot more squad cars looking for them. Perhaps now was the time to take her therapist's advice and risk believing in someone.

She needed to trust Ardal.

She took a deep breath. "What would you do in a situation where you were being hunted?"

The muscles in Ardal's jaw tightened. "Are you giving us permission to take action?"

"That depends on whether it's illegal." Jail wasn't her idea of a holiday.

"We kill only when necessary." Ardal spoke in a low voice. "I do not know what is criminal here."

"Fair enough." She knew what happened in the next few minutes would change her life forever. Fate was rushing at her headlong and she was incapable of stopping it.

"Please get us out of this mess."

"You will not hinder us?"

Fiona started to shake her head and then stopped. "Tell me I won't regret this."

"You will be safe."

"Not quite the same thing." Fiona bit her lip and then nodded. "Do what you have to. I won't interfere and I'll try to help if possible."

Ardal nodded. "Jehon. Find a new vehicle."

Within minutes Jehon had pulled off onto a side road and parked the truck. "I will return shortly."

The darkness of the night enclosed them. Fiona opened her mouth to speak and Ardal put a finger over it. Her eyes opened wide and she looked over to see what the problem was, but he wasn't looking at her. He was watching something in the darkness.

Surely Hunters couldn't see in the dark.

Jehon took ten minutes to return. He tapped on the truck window and then started grabbing stuff from the back of the truck bed. Fiona jumped out of the vehicle and stretched her body. The tension of waiting had seeped into her muscles. Would anything in her life be normal again?

Jehon was bent over the front of the truck and it took her few seconds to realize he was removing the license plates. How on earth had he figured they were a form of identification? She really hadn't given these guys enough credit.

She took her bag from Firbin and followed the men to a small widening in the road. An SUV was parked there. Within seconds, they were back on the highway. This time Fiona was sitting in the back with Firbin.

They drove with the headlights off.

"Can you guys see in the dark?" Fiona held the edge of her seat. They were going at least two times the speed limit.

"Our eyes have adapted." Ardal looked back at her. "You seem frightened."

"I am." The road was rushing by so fast that she was going to be sick. She shut her eyes. "You do realize that there are animals that sometimes cross the highway at night. If you hit something as big as a deer or a moose we could be killed."

"We can avoid it." Ardal glanced out the window before turning to Jehon. "Look for a place to spend the night."

Fiona breathed a sigh of relief. "A hotel sounds wonderful."

"We won't be staying inside." Ardal gave her a brief smile. "We are evading capture. We will stay away from places that would be easy to locate. I am assuming these hotels are at the edge of the road?"

"Yes." Fiona crossed her arms and leaned back in the seat. There was no point in arguing. Comfort was something they wouldn't understand.

"Your authorities would probably search there first."

Fiona glanced out the window before shutting her eyes. "Wake me when we're there."

The world whizzed by, as sleep escaped her. The men must have thought she was napping because they were talking in their own language. It had a musical quality about it.

About an hour later the vehicle turned off the road and started down what was little better than a cart track. The road jostled and bumped her around until she was bruised. They came to a stop after about five miles.

Ardal stepped out and motioned for the rest to stay. He walked into the dense forest and disappeared.

"Will we have to wait long?" Fiona couldn't keep the panic from her voice. She hated the dark, and the uncertainty of what was happening. Old fears were hard to put away. Even worse, she had anxiety about being separated from Ardal.

"Ardal is the finest Hunter and leader of all. The Kaladin high council trusted him to protect them. Few Hunters were given such honors." Jehon's voice was a low whisper.

"So he's good?"

"The truest." Firbin's voice held a note of reverence. "He is the only Hunter to fight the extinction orders. He brings honor with everything he does."

"You guys live and breathe that stuff." Fiona shook her head. "We don't have that."

"You no longer have warriors?" Firbin sounded incredulous.

"We have soldiers, and they have their own code. Our society doesn't live and breathe honor, though." Fiona shrugged.

Just then Ardal pulled the door open. "Move the vehicle into the trees and cover it."

They took the blankets, an axe, and the weapons from the truck. Fiona grabbed her bag and they started into the wilderness. There was no moon. The stars shone bright, but she had trouble walking on the uneven ground. She stumbled and tripped a couple of times before Ardal gave her his arm for support.

They walked for at least thirty minutes before the sound of water stopped them. Ardal led them up the side of a rocky outcrop. They were on solid bedrock.

When they reached a small overhang of rocks, they stopped. Ardal went in first and then motioned them to follow.

"This will keep us away from their equipment."

Fiona's eyes widened. "You really did learn a lot from that helicopter."

"It was primitive." Jehon's voice was dry.

"Always assume your enemy has better." Ardal kicked stones so there was a smooth area. "It would be best not to make a fire. Will you be able to stay warm tonight?"

"I'll be fine."

Ardal spread out one of the blankets and waited for her to lie on it before giving her another for covering. "Firbin get rest. Jehon check the supplies."

Ardal went to the front of the overhang. "I will take the first watch."

Chapter 11

She trusted him.

Exhilaration made his heart pound with purpose. Fiona had given him full control to protect her. Ardal looked out at the dark night and marveled at the sense of relief he felt. His years of training and breeding could be used for a cause that he wanted.

His men would be safe on this planet also. The atmosphere was giving them an advantage. They moved faster and their hits were harder. His vision was sharper, his hearing more acute, and he could smell Fiona's presence before he could see her.

His attraction to her was overwhelming.

The hold she had on him was terrifying.

For the first time in his life he wanted to touch a woman and feel her body shiver against his. He took a sharp breath as he remembered the shock of awareness that had passed between them when they touched. His heart had soared when she had examined him for injuries and rested her head on his chest. No one had ever cared if a Hunter were wounded or killed.

When that biker had held her captive, a surge of anger and pain had gripped him. He had wanted to lash out and destroy the man. He could not have borne it if harm had come to her. He had felt her fear. Her thoughts, even though unclear, had been in his mind. It was then that he had known the truth.

He heard the sure footfall of Jehon approaching. "Report."

"There is some foodstuff. We can hunt whatever else we need."

"There is plenty on this planet." Ardal's voice was indifferent. A Hunter could go days without food.

"The rules are different." Jehon's voice was cautious. "I am uncertain about this place."

"We have no choice." There was no gain by letting his men know his own concerns. "This is our home now. A Hunter does not fail."

"The woman is illogical." Jehon cleared his throat. "She does not know how to rule."

Ardal glanced at the man. "Her planet does not respect women. Fiona has proven herself to be knowledgeable and brave."

Jehon nodded. "Our bodies are responding unusually also."

"Explain."

"At first I thought it was our implants, but that is not the case." Jehon cleared his throat. "They have been deactivated."

Ardal looked at Jehon for a few seconds and then sighed. "You are certain."

Jehon nodded. "I have scanned mine and it is non-functioning."

"When were they shut down?"

"I suspect since we were captured on Cygnus." Jehon grimaced. "The Holman would not have wanted us strong."

"True." Ardal frowned. "Explain our increased abilities."

"It must be the planet's atmosphere and gravity that is causing the improvements." Jehon waved his hand in the air. "Our bodies travel faster, and our weight carries more strength."

"That is good. It will help us survive here."

Ardal looked up at the night sky. Stars glittered and sparkled in the cool air, making the sky a veritable sea of lights. Somewhere was the home where he had been born and trained, where he had fought and watched comrades die. All were lost.

They had a new world.

They would live and thrive.

"The others have reported similar changes." Jehon spoke in a lower voice. "We have a problem, though."

"You are full of good news this night." Ardal's voice was wry.

"We are traveling with a female." Jehon hesitated a second before continuing. "Our normal biological urges are not under the implant's control."

"Is it unbearable for you?" Ardal turned back to his comrade. His own awareness of Fiona was making him doubt his vows as a warrior.

"She is irrational and frustrating, yet at the same time you are happy to be near her." Jehon shook his head. "That has never happened before."

"Are you feeling anything else?"

"She is very beautiful." Jehon frowned. "This is the first time I have been aware of a woman's looks."

"No attraction?"

Jehon shook his head. "No. It is difficult to concentrate because of her nonsensical conversation. In the past, I would not have noticed. Do you think it will get worse?"

Ardal clenched his jaw. He knew how much worse it could get. "We will learn to deal with our awareness of women."

"The implants must be removed." Jehon's voice was decisive. "They could be used to track us."

Ardal sighed and looked back up at the sky. "I will make the others aware of the possible problems."

"Everyone is still safe?"

Ardal nodded. "Darrogh and his team have found a vehicle and are traveling non-stop to the destination. They are aware of our situation. If need be, they will create a diversion."

Just then the sound of a low flying craft was heard. Both men moved back into the rock overhang and waited. The vehicle was a helicopter and it moved over their area in a quick circle before turning back in a wider search radius. There were lights beaming down to the ground.

"They search for us." Ardal glanced back into the shelter.

"Their equipment will not be able to locate us through the rock." Jehon crossed his arms. "Their technology is limited."

"It matters not; we left witnesses at that eating place. We must travel without incident if we hope to blend in."

"There was no choice."

"No." Ardal watched the light of the helicopter fade as its search pattern widened. "Fiona needed defending. We will take better care in the future."

"Is it wise to continue traveling with her?" Jehon's voice had lowered to a whisper. "Perhaps it would be best for her to leave us."

"We have given our word." Ardal wiped his hand over his face. "She needs our protection."

"Her beauty is distinctive and memorable."

"True." How honest could he be with his men? He owed it to them, yet he could not abandon Fiona. Even if he forgot his vow and the Sacred Code, he could not leave her.

Knowing that the enhancers had been deactivated made his suspicions a certainty. He was bound to Fiona. No other living Hunter had ever experienced this. It was something no true warrior would have wanted.

"We should go in separate directions." Ardal straightened his shoulders and walked to the edge of the rock overhang. The cooler air was a balm against the heat that pulsed through him at the thought of Fiona. "Do you wish to join one of the other teams?"

"We can continue with the three of us." Jehon followed him.

"Fiona stays with me." Ardal's words were decisive.

"We risk capture."

"That is why I will not command you and Firbin to stay. In the morning you leave in the vehicle. Fiona and I will follow on foot."

"She will be safer on her own. Being with us is dangerous." Jehon's voice was earnest. "You are the last leader; a warrior honored and feared by the Kaladin and Holman alike. It is necessary for you to survive."

"Your words inspire me, but there are others who can lead if I do not survive." Ardal let a faint smile touch his lips. His decision to fight for their freedom had been right. No matter what happened, he would be remembered for that.

"You are wrong." Jehon stepped closer. "You gave us the chance to live again."

"And that is as it should be." He sighed. The truth was the only thing that would convince Jehon. "I cannot leave Fiona."

"I do not understand."

"There is no comprehending." He grasped Jehon's shoulder. "I am already bonded to her."

Jehon inhaled sharply. "Say it is not so."

"It is true."

"I thought bonding was a myth. It was told to us as children to keep us fearful of living without the implants."

"It is real." Ardal tightened his grip on Jehon. "It is not to be dreaded, either."

"It takes a leader from us." Jehon's voice was low with horror.

"I have gone nowhere." He leaned close to Jehon. "I am the same as before, but there is a connection with Fiona. I feel her fears and understand her needs. Soon her thoughts will be clear to me."

Jehon straightened. "I will stay. No matter the risk. You cannot face this alone."

"I can defend myself. I will make my decision for our travel in the morning." Ardal motioned back to the shelter. "Sleep. Your watch will be here soon enough."

Jehon nodded and went inside. Ardal was left with the night and his thoughts. He walked to the edge of the rock ledge. The helicopter had long since left. Jehon had been right. They would be more noticeable traveling as a foursome. The best decision would be to divide.

He would travel with Fiona. There was no choice. He was connected to her.

Bonded.

He heaved a sigh. Throughout his whole life, he had believed that bonding was a myth. To lose control and be at the whim of fate was abhorrent to a Hunter. To be enslaved and tied to another was a curse. A Hunter lived for duty and honor; there was no room for a mate. Now he knew the truth.

Fiona was his pair bond.

He did not fear it, though. He was connected to her in an indescribable way. Nothing had prepared him for it. His first sense of attraction had seemed a reaction to the ordeal of the crash, but it was more than that. He had felt Fiona's horror and terror during the fight with the bikers. Her fears were a reality to him. He had fought the urge to hold and soothe her.

If legend were true, death could not sever the connection. He would only desire the one he was bonded to. That would be his fate. There was no understanding of why one was chosen over another. Some said it was a word, a glance, or a gesture that sealed one's destiny. For him it had been all those things, but the shock of awareness that spread through his body when they touched had been the real sign.

One bonding.

One mate.

The Holman had claimed that bad genetic script and the mutations that had been used to give them strength, persistence, competitiveness, and endurance had caused the problem. The chromosomal alterations had amplified their focus and intensity, but had narrowed and deepened their mating urges until they would choose only one. Genetic engineering had made them invincible warriors, but these same attributes reinforced their devotion and loyalty to their mate.

It was considered dangerous and treasonous for a Hunter to have a mate. He might choose her over his orders. The Kaladin would not tolerate this. Eons ago, it was decided that Hunters would never mate and to ensure this, they all had implants at birth to prevent it.

Now the implants had been deactivated and he was the first to experience the bonding.

It was ironic. He had chosen to disobey a direct order and he would be the first to suffer the consequences. His men would have to be warned. They would find it hard to understand, but they would accept that he might have other considerations when making decisions. It would be up to them whether he remained their leader.

Five hours into his watch Ardal had notified his men of the situation. They had been surprised, but wanted him to remain as leader.

The night had grown cold by the time he woke Jehon to relieve him. Jehon yawned and then stood.

"You have told them?" Jehon's voice was a low whisper.

Ardal nodded. "They are aware."

"What is your decision?"

"In the morning you and Firbin travel without us."

Jehon nodded. "I will take watch."

Ardal turned to sit down when Fiona's voice stopped him. "Is it time to wake?"

"No. We are changing watch." Ardal picked up Jehon's blanket."

"I'm cold."

Her voice was husky with sleep and tugged at his previously dormant heart. There was no combating the need to please her. He snapped the blanket open and walked to where she lay. He spread it over her.

Her voice was low, but audible. "Stay."

Chapter 12

"That is not wise." Ardal's whisper echoed through the cave.

"I need you." Fiona didn't care how illogical it was; having Ardal near kept the panic away.

With a grunt, he lay beside her. He pulled her close and wrapped the blanket around both of them. His body heat warmed her. It melted away the shock of the last twenty-four hours. She snuggled her head high on his chest and snaked her hand up under his shirt. Soft whorls of hair brushed her fingers before she reached his heart. It beat strong and steady.

"Better?" Ardal's voice was husky.

She sighed. "I feel safe."

"Then I am content." Ardal's arm tightened around her. "I will not leave you."

"I know."

It was crazy, but deep inside she knew it was the truth. Any other man who had killed with such precision and calm would have terrified her, but not Ardal. His every action had been to keep her safe. Even now, tired and in need of sleep, he had given her what she needed.

"Thank you," she mumbled before sleep claimed her once again.

It was several hours later when faint light filtered through to the rear of the cave. Fiona blinked her eyes in protest. With a groan she twisted her head on her pillow, frowning at the warmth pouring from it. It felt like a furnace. The rest of her body was stiff. With a start she realized that she wasn't sleeping on a bed, but bedrock. Her hand stretched and explored the heat beneath her head.

"Dangerous."

With a gasp she looked up.

Ardal.

Fiona winced. Heat flooded her face as she lifted her head from his chest. "I'm sorry." Her voice was barely a squeak.

"No need." Ardal sat up. "You were cold."

"Thank you." Fiona pushed her hair off her face and grimaced as she tried to sit. Every bone in her body ached. "Did someone beat me last night?" she groaned.

"No one touched you." Ardal's voice was firm.

"I was joking." She sat and stretched her arms over her head. "Where are the others?"

"Firbin is on watch and Jehon has gone to hunt."

She pushed off her blanket and stood. "I have energy bars in my pack."

"Save them until it is necessary." Ardal stood and took the blanket from her. "We need to conserve our supplies."

"But we'll reach Toronto this afternoon." Fiona's eyes narrowed as she watched Ardal's face. Something was different. The man refused to look her in the eye and he was making damn certain that he didn't touch her.

"What's happened?"

He shook his head. "Our plans must change. Your military was looking for us last night."

"And you let me sleep?" Horror and anger surged through her. What if they'd been found? God, was she ever going to feel safe again?

"I will protect you." Ardal's quiet voice broke into her thoughts. "You said that you would trust me to make the right decisions."

"I do." She shook her head. How had he known what she was feeling? Was she that obvious?

Ardal touched her arm and again that shock of electricity raced through her body. "Do you need privacy?"

It took a second for her to realize what he was asking. She gave him a slight smile. After all her efforts to make them understand last night, this was a welcome change.

"I'll find a tree or something."

He frowned. "I do not understand."

"We're camping." Fiona walked to the overhang. "It's not like we have indoor plumbing."

Ardal shrugged and pointed to a path that led down to the water. "I will meet you there."

Fiona found the cover of a cedar and took care of her morning business. When she was finished she took stock of their surroundings. They were on a high rock outcrop. It was a great hiding place. You could see anyone coming at you from miles away. She had to hand it to these Hunters. They knew what they were doing.

When she reached the water, Jehon and Firbin were there also. They looked up as she approached. There was a small fire near the water's edge and fish on sticks were being cooked over it. Ardal retrieved one of them and brought it to her.

"Eat."

"So much for morning conversation." Fiona sat on a rock and started to pick the meat off the stick. It was surprisingly delicious with a smoky taste.

"We have made plans." Ardal sat beside her. "Firbin's leg is much improved. He and Jehon will take the vehicle. You and I will go by foot. We will find another way to Toronto."

"Is that safe?"

"They will be looking for three men and a woman. You will be recognized. " Ardal cleared his throat. "Also, you are a distraction."

"You mean because I can't make up my mind."

Ardal looked at Jehon and then back to her. "You are a woman and that makes it difficult for us to focus."

"You said you weren't affected by that kind of stuff."

"Our implants are deactivated." Jehon spoke in a tight voice. He held a knife that he was heating in the fire. "We are as normal men now."

"And that bothers you?"

"It is not something we have dealt with in the past." Ardal nodded to Jehon. "We need to focus on fitting into this world."

So there it was. Fiona heaved a sigh and blew the hair from her face. "Drop me off at the nearest town. I'll get a bus."

"No." Ardal held his left arm out to Jehon. "You and I will travel together."

Fiona frowned as she watched Jehon bring the heated knife to Ardal's skin. "What the heck are you doing?"

"Removing the implant." Jehon felt Ardal's forearm with a finger and then plunged the knife in.

Ardal's jaw tightened but no sound escaped him. Was the man made of stone? Just as the thought raced through her mind, he looked at her. She saw the fire and pain in his eyes and gasped. He knew what she was thinking. His gaze was fixed on her so that she was the only one who could see his suffering.

She bit her lip and forced back the nausea. His distress was hers. She couldn't take her eyes from him. How could he stand the burning, searing probe of the knife? Just when she was going to shout for Jehon to stop, he pulled the knife out. A small metal object came away with the blade. Ardal released the breath he'd been holding.

"Are you insane?" Fiona's voice shook with shock. "A doctor should have taken that out."

"There is no time." Ardal pressed his hand against the wound. "We cannot risk the implant being activated."

Fiona scrambled to his side. She ripped a strip off her shirt and pressed it against the wound. "Someone get my bag."

Firbin ran back to the cave and returned a minute later. He threw the bag over to her and she rummaged in it until she found a small first aid kit. She found the antibacterial lotion and a bandage. "It needs a stitch."

"It will heal."

She shook her head and went to cleaning and closing the wound as best she could. "Are you all going to do this?"

"Yes."

"At least I'll be prepared."

She looked into Ardal's dark eyes. She saw understanding and gratitude there. A surge of warmth flowed through her and centered in her heart. This man affected her in a way that she had never experienced before. She exhaled a shaky breath and forced her gaze away.

When Jehon went to use the knife on Firbin, she intervened. Despite their skill, her medical training gave her an edge. She found the implant and with deft assurance sliced and removed it with half the damage Jehon had inflicted on Ardal. She did Jehon next. When both of the men were bandaged she put the knife back in the fire along with the implants.

"Are you safe now?"

"The Holman will not be able to track us." Ardal pulled on his hoodie. "If they learn that the ship crashed, they might search for survivors. It is best they think us dead."

"What about the others?" Fiona pulled the knife from the fire and brushed the charcoal on her jeans. "Won't they be at risk, too?"

"They know to remove the implants." Ardal picked up the small baggie that had held the first aid kit. He filled it up with water and splashed it on the fire.

Fiona opened her mouth to ask how when she was caught by Ardal's glance. It was intense and warning. She shrugged. It was no big secret. These guys had a hidden communication system like mobile phones. She frowned. That didn't make sense though. Phones required a cellular system to work off. Perhaps they'd tapped into one of the cell towers.

"It's not safe to use phones." Fiona blurted the words before thinking. Ardal raised an eyebrow. "I just don't want you guys caught. It's my fault that all of this is happening."

"You did not cause us to crash." It was Firbin who spoke in a low voice. "You have only tried to help."

"If I hadn't insisted that we stop to eat, you'd be in Toronto right now."

"It is done." Ardal's voice was firm. "We must leave."

Just like that, the military leader was back. Fiona stood and watched the wheels of command take over. Any second now and she'd have expected the men to salute. He had an easy way of directing, though. Before long they had broken camp and were standing by the stolen car. Firbin seemed to hesitate when it came to separating.

"It is for the best." Ardal opened the SUV door. "You need to recover. Your skills are needed."

"I would risk it."

"I will not." Ardal pushed the younger man into the vehicle. "That is why I am in command."

Firbin sighed. "Hunters true and right."

"By Cygnus and Warrior we will meet again."

No further words were spoken. The vehicle drove down the rough path to the highway. Within seconds it was out of sight. Silence surrounded them. Fiona rubbed her arms, trying to suppress the sense of isolation and loneliness that she felt.

"I will not leave." Ardal's voice was quiet and sincere. "We need to move."

They had already cleaned the cave area and hidden the evidence of their campfire. Ardal carried a pack fashioned out of their blankets, which held most of their supplies. Fiona slung her backpack over her shoulder.

As they left the area, Ardal took branches and covered their tracks. They avoided the soft ground and walked along the stony shoreline for at least two miles before cutting inland toward the highway. By the time they reached the road's edge, it was well past noon.

Fiona was exhausted and her feet hurt. At this rate, they'd be in Toronto next year. She groaned when Ardal moved back into the treeline. It made sense to stay hidden, but the land was harder to navigate and the branches had already cut her arms to pieces. She wasn't even counting the number of mosquito and blackfly bites she had.

Ardal stopped without warning. "You are tired. We will rest here."

Fiona tried to deny it, but her mouth refused to work. She sat down with a thud and pulled out her water bottle. "How long do we have to do this?"

Ardal shrugged. "Until we are safe."

"How will you know?" She didn't hide her sarcasm. "You're not exactly familiar with how things work here."

"Staying hidden and on the move is the same no matter what planet you are on." Ardal sat beside her. "Instinct and training will keep us alive."

"Have you done this for long?"

"Since I could walk." Ardal wet a small piece of cloth and held it to her neck. "This will cool you down. We will camp soon."

"Isn't it a bit early?"

Ardal looked up at the sun. "I want to travel at night."

Great. Fiona sighed. "You can see in the dark."

Ardal smiled. "This planet has given my senses an edge, but I do not have night vision. There are no clouds, so this evening should be as bright as last night."

Fiona looked up. He was right about the clear sky. Still, night was cold and the animals were out then. A shiver of dread ran up her back. What if they came across a pack of wolves?

"What are wolves?"

Fiona's head swung back to Ardal. "How did you do that?"

"I did nothing." Ardal's eyes glanced away from her.

Suddenly it was clear. These men had abilities that she could only guess at. She'd made the mistake of underestimating them. They looked human so she'd thought of them as being the same as her. That was obviously not the case.

"You can hear our thoughts." Fiona jumped up waving her hands about her head. "No wonder you don't need a phone. You have built in antennae just like the old movies of little green men from Mars."

Chapter 13

Ardal considered not answering, but that was cowardly. He was a well-decorated warrior; an elite Hunter. He had no need to hide or pretend. His word was respected. Why then did he have a sinking feeling in the pit of his stomach?

Her voice reverberated in his head. He was experiencing every emotion she felt. Fear, anger, curiosity, and uncertainty all surged through Fiona. He did not understand some of her words, but the meaning was clear. She thought he had a mechanical instrument that allowed him to hear thoughts.

"You are wrong." Ardal kept his voice quiet. She was already overexcited. Calm and direct honesty was what she needed right now. "I am only beginning to understand your thoughts. I started sensing your emotions when I first saw you."

"Do you do this everywhere you go?"

"No." Ardal took her arm and eased her back down. "Since arriving on your planet we have been experiencing many strange things."

"How do I know that you're telling me the truth?"

"A Hunter does not lie."

"That's part of your Sacred Code I suppose?" Fiona crossed her arms. "I knew you were keeping things from me."

"I have not told you any falsehoods." Ardal leaned close. "My secrets will be yours."

This was not strictly true. He was forbidden from telling all. Even a commander such as himself could not reveal that he was able to communicate with his men by mind connection. No one other than a Hunter knew that.

"How did you know that I was thinking about wolves?"

"It is part of the bonding." Ardal kept his voice devoid of emotion.

Fiona's eyes widened and she put up her hand defensively. "I don't want any man hearing my thoughts."

"Then you can close them to me." A sharp pain twisted in his chest at the thought of her denying him this most intimate of communication. Even if they never took the step that would make them mates, legend said that bonded pairs kept their channel of connection open.

"You're sure that I can do that?"

"Positive." Ardal cleared his throat. "You should know that it would make it impossible for me to know when you were in danger, though."

Fiona tilted her head. "Is that why you can connect to me? You're worried about my safety?"

"Yes. In our culture we have legends of two people connecting in such a way. We call it bonding. Up until we landed on your planet, I thought that it was a myth."

"So you've never experienced this before."

Ardal shook his head. "No."

"Do the others know what I think and feel?" Fiona's hands flitted restlessly on her lap.

Ardal shook his head. "It is only between the pair bond."

"I suppose it gives us an advantage. If I was in trouble then you'd know it." Fiona hands twisted together. "Still, I don't like it. I should have traveled alone."

"You helped us at great danger to yourself. You are my responsibility and I will protect you."

"I appreciate you trying." Fiona raised her hand to his cheek and stroked down the stubble of his beard. Her fingers lingered at the corner of his mouth and she shook her head. He sensed that she was going to argue.

He turned and kissed her fingers. A piercing bolt of desire raced through his body knocking the air from his lungs. Never had he experienced such a thing. Only Fiona's sharply inhaled breath told him that she felt it too.

"This is insane," she whispered. "What was that?"

"Our bond is strengthening." Ardal's voice was hoarse.

Her touch had a power that he had never felt before. It was stronger than any natural force or weapon. Fiona's tongue flicked over her lower lip and for the first time in his life he wondered how a woman would taste. Not just any woman, though. Fiona was the only one he wanted.

He pulled her close and with his free hand brushed her hair from her face. By Cygnus, she was beautiful. He glanced down at her lips and was lost. Lowering his head, he captured her mouth. Thoughts scattered as sensation took over. His tongue glided over her lips. He licked and nibbled until she sighed and opened for him.

He thrust into the warm, moist haven she offered. His body hardened and control was forgotten as he delved deeper, skimming his tongue against hers, soothing and sliding until bliss spread over him. A surge of longing and need shot through him and concentrated in his groin.

Her scent filled his nostrils and the pounding of her heart was music to his ears. His hands roamed her back, but her shirt blocked a total bonding. With shaking fingers he pulled the cotton fabric from her jeans and then buried his hand beneath it. He connected with the silky smoothness of her skin and his body sizzled with intense yearning.

Never had he felt such pleasure. It was overwhelming. Fiona seemed to be experiencing the same because her body moved against him with frantic impatience. Desire, hunger, concern, and reverence all battled inside of him. Fiona was his pair bond. She deserved better than a hurried mating. He had to end this now.

A groan of conscious escaped him and he pulled away. He had to do what was best for Fiona. She needed time; time to trust him and time to commit to him. She looked up at him, her eyes glazed with passion. His breathing was too rapid to speak. He rested his forehead against hers and tried to recover. His body shook, his groin ached, and his brain refused to focus, but he had his answer.

Fiona tasted of heaven.

"Wow." Fiona moved away.

"I should not have touched you."

"It took me by surprise." Fiona tucked her shirt back into her jeans."

"I believe it's rare to have such a powerful connection."

"Good thing." Fiona shook her head. "I'm not sure a person could handle that much intensity for long."

Ardal stood. He was acting like a raw recruit. He had let his attraction to Fiona override his judgement. His only excuse was a lack of experience with bonding. In the future, he would guard against temptation.

"We need to move. Once you are safe, then the need to connect will not be so strong."

"That's probably it." Fiona seemed glad to accept his explanation. She jumped up and waited for him to lead the way.

"You have not explained wolves."

"They're animals, sort of like dogs. They hunt in packs and some people think that they will attack for no reason."

"Picture one in your head."

She looked at him blankly for a second and then nodded. She didn't disappoint. Within seconds an image of an animal with long fur and brilliant eyes appeared in his mind. Soon there were others and they all moved together.

"This creature will not be a problem." Ardal started to walk. "I have seen similar beasts on other planets. Usually only hunger will bring them close."

"Let's hope so," Fiona muttered as she fell into step behind him.

He kept to the woods, skirting close to the edge so that the highway was in site. He didn't want to deviate too far from civilization. His goal was to commandeer a vehicle and finish the journey. He knew Fiona was unused to this much walking. Soon, she would be unable to move.

Another mile later, they were rewarded by the appearance of a small gas station. It had a restaurant attached and Fiona looked at it with longing.

"We might get help there." Her voice was eager.

"They will know we walked." Ardal frowned. There did not seem to be any means of leaving the place either. Only one car stood in front of the building. "It will be noticed if we borrow that one."

"We'll tell them that ours broke down." Fiona was almost hopping with excitement. "They might know how we can get another, or if a bus stops nearby."

"What is a bus?"

"A long vehicle that drives people to places for money." Fiona started to walk out of the woods. "They're not the most comfortable, but it's better than walking. I doubt the police will look for us in one."

Ardal could not deny her enthusiasm. Staying hidden was the safest route, but Fiona could not walk much further. It was against his training to risk being seen, but he needed to consider Fiona. If there was a problem, he would deal with it.

He nodded. "Stay close to me," he cautioned before starting across the highway.

A bell jingled when they entered the restaurant. Ardal looked around the nearly deserted place. There were only four other people in the room. One was behind a counter and the other three were seated together at a table in the corner. He noticed the same sign as the other restaurant which had indicated a washroom. At least Fiona would not have to use a bush this time.

"Sit where ever you want folks." The man behind the counter pointed to the empty tables. "You're lucky to beat the rush hour."

The other people started to laugh. He walked to a table near the far end. He sat with his back against the wall. Fiona started to follow him but changed her mind when she saw the washroom sign. He hid his smile. It was a simple thing, yet he knew that she was pleased.

Ardal's eyes narrowed as he noticed the three diners who were men, watching Fiona walk away. Their eyes followed her every move and he could sense that it made her uncomfortable. He clenched his hands. It was wrong that she felt threatened by these strangers.

The man from the counter came over with glasses of water and menus. "You folks traveling far?"

Ardal nodded and reached for the menu. "Our vehicle broke down a few miles back."

"That explains the little lady's forlorn look." The man shook his head. "The sooner she rests, the better it'll be for you."

The men from the other table started laughing. Ardal frowned. He glanced at them. They grinned back and nodded. One of them raised a glass in his direction.

"No sense in angering them unnecessarily."

"Speak for yourself." A second man poked the first. "A bit of spark and fury makes for a more interesting life."

The first man started laughing. "That's why you're on your third wife, Ralph."

"Hey, I never said it was perfect, but at least I've got sparks in bed."

"I like a woman that keeps the peace." The third man took a sip of coffee. "Then gives me a piece later."

The men were still laughing when Fiona came out of the washroom. She gave them a quick glance and then rushed over to Ardal. He sensed her panic and took her hand as she sat down. She smiled. He made no attempt to read her thoughts. He would wait until she was comfortable with the pair bonding.

"Those men make me nervous." Fiona leaned close to him. "Did you ask the owner about a vehicle yet?"

Ardal handed her a menu. "Are you hungry?"

Fiona sighed and took the menu. "Who knows when we'll be able to sit down for a meal?"

Ardal pushed away from the table. "I will speak to the man now about a vehicle."

Fiona put her hand on his. "Wait."

Before he could say anything the man from the counter returned. Fiona ordered for both of them before asking for a vehicle.

"Not much around here." The man scratched his head. "Closest place to rent would be North Bay."

"How far?" Ardal's voice was sharper than he had intended.

"You're a couple of hours away at least."

Fiona sighed. "Does the bus come through here?"

"Regular as clockwork." The man motioned to the counter. "I'll have to phone ahead for you if you want to pick it up. They don't usually stop."

Fiona gave the man a bright smile. "Could you do that, please?"

The man seemed to be at a loss of words at first and then nodded. "Right away. It'll be at least an hour before it comes by."

Ardal watched the man walk away and felt a flicker of sympathy. He knew how devastating Fiona's smile could be. "Do we have enough money?"

Fiona nodded. "The first rule of life on the run is to have a substantial emergency kit with enough cash."

"Emergency kit?"

"Anyone hiding has to have something ready in case they have to leave in a hurry." Fiona took a sip of water. "You never know when you'll have to take off."

"Or when aliens will crash in your field?" Ardal couldn't resist the tease and was rewarded with a smile. The knot of anxiety he felt over her eased. She would be fine.

They ate their meal in silence. No words were needed. The bus had been notified and would make the stop to pick them up. All was settled for now. They had just finished their coffee when Ardal sensed Fiona stiffen beside him. He looked up and saw her look of horror. She was staring out the window. He followed her eyes and understood.

A police car had just pulled up outside the restaurant. Ardal leaned back in his chair and assessed the easiest route for escape. He would have no problem overpowering the men at the other table. The man behind the counter would probably duck down. That left the policeman. From what Fiona had told him, he would be armed.

His eyes narrowed as he watched the officer enter the restaurant. The man pushed his hat back on his head. "Morning Bill," he said to the man behind the counter. He then looked at the other men and nodded. "You boys ever work?"

"Not if we can help it." A laugh went up from the men. "You're a fine one to be talking Jim. I swear you're here more than on patrol."

The officer grinned. "You never know where you'll find trouble." Then he looked over at them.

He hesitated a second and then walked to their table. Fiona tensed beside him and Ardal went into combat mode. When the attack came he would be ready.

"Are you folks traveling south?"

Ardal nodded. "We are waiting for the bus."

"You wouldn't know about some trouble up the road with the FD Warriors?"

"We're not from here, officer." Fiona spoke in a quiet voice. "Is there something we should know?"

"Seems like a bunch of bikers disappeared outside of Timmins." The policeman tapped his fingers against his belt. "They were seen arguing with some awfully big men."

"How horrible." Fiona shifted in her chair.

Ardal felt her eyes on him, but he kept his focus on the officer. The man's gaze flitted over him with speculation before turning to Fiona. Ardal leaned back in his chair and eased his hand closer to his weapon.

"They were fighting over a red headed girl."

"That sounds like a place to avoid." Ardal forced his voice to remain calm.

"I couldn't help noticing your girlfriend's red hair." The officer swayed back on his heels. "It's a bit distinctive. Where were you two coming from?"

Chapter 14

"Are you accusing me of something?" Fiona's voice rose. "There are a lot of women with red hair.

The officer raised his hands. "I'm just warning you to be careful. That gang doesn't forget a face or a deed done against them. It would be a shame if you were mistaken for the one they're looking for."

Fiona forced herself to steady her breathing. She'd thought they were caught and she'd reacted with screeching. Her normal calm and logical self had been replaced with an hysterical, unreasonable witch. How had she come to this?

She forced a smile. "I'm having a rough day. First the car broke down, then the walk here, and now this."

"I understand ma'am." The officer lowered his voice. "I'd be careful just the same. Even though you're not the one these bikers are looking for, there's no saying that they won't make trouble because they've lost face."

"She is safe with me." Ardal spoke with a quiet authority.

Her heart flipped as his voice sent a wave of peace through her. Of course she was safe. Hadn't he already proven he was capable of protecting her? She reached across the table and touched his hand. The familiar surge of heat raced through her body and calmed her.

"You look like you could handle yourself." The cop had turned his attention to Ardal. "You do any wrestling?"

Ardal shook his head. "I was a soldier."

"That explains it." The officer readjusted his hat and nodded as he turned away. "Is that coffee ready Bill?"

Relief flooded Fiona. Unless they had pictures of them, they were safe. Besides it didn't sound as if there were any arrests to be made in the case. It was more a matter of the bikers wanting revenge.

"What is losing face?" Ardal pushed back his chair and gave her the backpack.

"It's when you're embarrassed because someone wiped the floor with you."

Ardal raised an eyebrow. "That makes even less sense."

He leaned close and she felt his breath against her ear. She inhaled sharply, letting him invade her senses. She was dizzy with the scent of him. She looked into his eyes and saw her own helplessness reflected there. He was as affected as she was. The slam of the restaurant door broke the spell.

"We should go." Her voice caught in her throat. "The bus will be here soon."

Ardal waited at the door while she paid for their meal and the bus tickets. Once they were outside, she took a gulp of fresh air.

"That place needed air conditioning."

"You found it hot?" Ardal pulled the hood of his sweatshirt up.

"Not really." Fiona kicked a few stones with her foot. "I didn't like the way those men looked at me."

"Neither did I." Ardal glanced back at the restaurant. "Are all men on this planet disrespectful?"

"Who knows?" Fiona sighed. "So far my experience has been pretty limited. Except for David, I only had a couple of boyfriends in university."

"You did not find a mate?"

"I was too busy studying." Fiona pulled her hair back with both hands. "Do you think that policeman suspected anything?"

Ardal pulled her close. "There is no need to panic. I am a Hunter. I protect."

Fiona grimaced. "You're always covering up for me. I'm sorry that you guys are in this mess. If I'd handled the biker better, we'd have been in Toronto by now."

"We will get there." Ardal ran a finger down her cheek and patted her lips. "You must not speak ill of yourself."

"I'm a mess." Fiona glanced up at him. "I overreacted with the policeman. I did the same with Captain Wilson. I must have a problem with uniforms."

"I will remember not to wear one." Ardal put his forehead on hers. "What is wrong with their attire?"

"It brings back bad memories." Fiona sighed. "I've talked to so many policemen about David and they could do nothing."

"Is not beating a woman illegal?"

"Yes, but he was clever. He never did it in front of anyone." Frustration and anger surged through her. "It was his word against mine. His friends always gave him an alibi. I thought I was crazy and the police wrote me off as a hysterical female who'd lie to get attention."

"You are not crazy."

"How can you be sure?" Fiona pushed away from him. "All I've done since meeting you is scream at people. I've caused nothing but trouble for you and your men."

Ardal lifted her chin with his forefinger. Her eyes collided with his. "Your action with the military meant that I was able to send Jehon and Firbin to the barn where they hid the Captain."

Fiona frowned. "I thought that I'd made matters worse."

Ardal shook his head. "You were perfect. Jehon was even able to sneak a look at the helicopter."

"What about the policeman?" Fiona shook her head. "I should never have yelled at him."

"You are still filled with fear." Ardal straightened his shoulders. "In time, you will realize that I will always defend you."

"What happens when you're not there?"

"I cannot leave you."

"Because you believe you're bonded to me?" Fiona rolled her eyes. "Once you see other women, you'll think differently."

"I do not control it." Ardal lowered his voice. "It is fated."

Fiona wanted to scoff at his insistence, but the sincerity in his eyes stopped her. He really believed it. Fate wouldn't have joined two people who, under normal circumstances should never have met. But why argue? Let him have his illusions. Once he saw other women, she was certain his attraction to her would be gone.

With a sigh she turned away and looked down the road. In the distance she saw the bus. She waved her arms. The sooner they got to Toronto, the better she'd breathe.

The bus was crowded. The smell of unwashed bodies was overwhelming, but Ardal didn't seem to notice. He looked about for two seats together, but there were none. For a second, she thought that he was going to throw someone out of their seat. Instead, he motioned her to sit near the front. He moved further down to the back.

It didn't really matter where she sat. She was exhausted. All she wanted was sleep. She sensed Ardal was unhappy about leaving her alone, but she was too tired to explain it. Instead she pulled her legs up close and closed her eyes.

She wasn't certain what woke her.

She sensed Ardal was upset, though.

She stretched and straightened in her seat. It took her eyes a few seconds to focus, because the sun was low in the sky. She must have slept for quite a few hours. The woman who had sat beside her was gone. She glanced at the passenger across the aisle and she was unfamiliar too.

Her unease was overwhelming.

She turned in her seat and looked to the rear of the bus. Ardal was standing and already walking up the aisle. He reached for her shoulder just as the bus jolted to a stop.

Her chest tightened and it hurt to breath. She reached for Ardal's hand on her shoulder. The bus driver opened the door and two soldiers with machine guns boarded. Her stomach dropped.

Before yesterday, she had never seen a machine gun.

Now she had seen five.

"Stay." Ardal's voice was a low hiss. "You do not know me."

The knot in her stomach twisted as Ardal walked to the front. There had to be some way to save him, but even as she started to leave her seat, his hand motioned her to stay. She couldn't let him walk away to what would be certain death. Her whole being rejected the possibility that she would never see him again.

Ardal didn't resist when the soldiers pushed him off the bus. Fiona released the breath she'd been holding. She'd expected him to overpower the men, despite the guns they wielded. For a few seconds, there was total silence and then everyone started talking at once except the bus driver. He turned and stared at her.

Seconds later, a soldier came onboard again.

He looked at her directly. It was pointless to fight. She'd probably broken some unknown immigration law about harboring aliens. Whatever the reason, the soldier wanted her to leave the bus.

With a sigh she stood and heaved her backpack over her shoulder. When she got to the front, the soldier motioned her down the steps where another gun waited to direct her toward a helicopter.

"I'm not getting in that thing." She dug her feet into the ground. "Besides, you haven't told me what I've done."

Another soldier stepped in front of her and she recognized Captain Wilson from the farm. "We'll start with lying to the government. That is treason."

"You've got to be kidding. You're grasping at straws."

"I know you're guilty." Wilson pushed her until they reached the helicopter's door. "We just need to hammer out the details."

"Is that a threat?" Ardal's voice was a low growl.

Fiona turned toward him. He was sitting in the helicopter with his hands handcuffed behind his back. Two soldiers were pointing machine guns at him. It made no sense, but even in the face of danger, the sight of him gave her peace.

"It's a promise." Wilson smirked. "You might have thought that you were pretty smart, but no one makes a fool of me."

"Believe this." Ardal leaned toward the Captain. "If you touch her, I will kill you."

There was a second of silence before Wilson swung the butt of his gun across Ardal's face. The sound of it reverberated in the cabin of the chopper. The other soldiers looked away quickly to cover their expressions of surprise and shock, but Fiona couldn't hold back. She kicked Wilson in the knee.

"Leave him alone." Then she slapped him across the face. "He can't even defend himself, you brute. When did this country become a military state?"

Wilson turned and snarled at her, his face inches away from hers. His eyes bulged with anger and his nostrils flared. Fiona took a step back. Wilson grabbed her arm and shook her.

One of the other soldiers put out his hand. "It's time we left, sir."

For the space of a heartbeat, she thought that the Captain was going to ignore the interruption. She held her breath and waited for the hit, but it didn't come. Instead Wilson backed away and nodded to his men.

"Put the handcuffs on her."

"What's the charge?"

"Treason."

Fiona's arms were grabbed and pulled behind her back. The cold metal sent a shiver up her arms and she clenched her fingers together. There was something wrong with a country that could use the military in such a manner. She looked over at Ardal and the icy stillness of his eyes sent a chill of dread through her body.

She was picked up and put in the seat beside him. He didn't look at her. Instead his eyes were focused on the Captain. She sensed a determination and readiness in him. He was a leopard waiting for his chance to strike.

She didn't want Ardal killed. She was certain the military wouldn't hesitate, though. All they wanted was to determine what he was. There were no restraints on how they went about that. Her heart constricted at the possible methods they would use.

Fiona already knew what he was.

He was a man she couldn't live without.

She let out a shaky breath and edged closer to Ardal. He didn't move or acknowledge her, but he didn't object either. There was only one place that was going to make her feel better. She put her head on his chest and closed her eyes.

"Well isn't that sweet." Wilson's words were meant to hurt, but they barely registered.

Fiona moved her head on Ardal's chest until she was comfortable. She didn't expect him to notice as he was so focused on their captors, but she almost cried when he rested his chin on her head. Peace and calm flowed through her.

Once the chopper took off there was no chance of conversation. Fiona refused to look at the soldiers. Their guns and attitude a reminder of the horror that she'd fled from. Men and their aggressions were why she was in this situation.

They flew over miles of wilderness. The helicopter hovered over the tree tops as it made its way north. She had no idea where they were headed, but when a clearing came into view with a number of buildings, she knew they'd arrived. It looked military in nature and old.

They landed and were met by four more armed soldiers. Fiona was lifted from the helicopter, but Ardal was pushed out. With his hands behind his back he was unbalanced, but kept on his feet. He was pushed from behind with their guns.

"Walk."

There were a couple of trucks and a jeep off to the side of the helipad, but that was all. Wilderness surrounded them. They were cut off from civilization and at the mercy of the military. The reality of their isolation sent a wave of terror through Fiona.

They were moved to a barrack-looking building. It was a steel curved hut with a layer of rust on it that had to be decades old. Once inside, the soldiers left them alone, except for Wilson. The Captain stayed at their side and waited. He was rewarded a couple of minutes later by the opening of the side door. Two officers entered.

"This is my commander Colonel White and this is Major Thomas. They are with military intelligence and have a few questions for you."

Wilson moved them forward and pushed them into chairs. "I'd suggest you be honest with them. You can start by telling us your real name."

"Why should I?" A year in hiding had taught her not to divulge anything.

"No problem." Wilson leaned into her face. "I'm certain your fingerprints will give us the information me need."

Fiona lifted her chin. "These cuffs are uncomfortable."

The Major nodded at Wilson and he undid them. She rubbed her wrists and grimaced at the soreness. She would have continued, but she noticed Ardal looking down at her. His face was impassive, but his eyes burned with anger. She put her hands between her knees and tried to smile.

"We've got a friend of yours." The Major walked to the side door and nodded.

A hooded man was led into the room and seated at a chair in front of them. He was also handcuffed. There was something familiar about his walk and clothing. Fiona looked up at Ardal, but his face remained blank. He would have made an excellent poker player.

The hood was lifted to reveal Captain Eamon.

"It seems that you forgot him when you decided to run." The Colonel laughed. "Not very smart, considering how much the Captain likes to talk."

"He has no honor." Ardal's voice was full of disdain.

"Perhaps, but he's been telling us a fascinating tale about you." Colonel White moved to stand in front of them. "It's General Ardal, if I'm not mistaken."

"It was rather careless of you to take the bus." Major Thomas leaned back against the table beside the chairs. "You can thank an astute policeman for your capture."

Captain Wilson snickered behind her. "He became suspicious when he didn't find an abandoned vehicle on the road."

Fiona closed her eyes and fought back her tears of frustration. It was her fault. Again. If she hadn't insisted on stopping, they'd still be free.

"You really should have been more accommodating," Wilson whispered in her ear. "When we're done, you'll be begging for death."

Chapter 15

Ardal buried his anger. He replaced it with cold calculating focus. It was the same focus that had kept him alive through twenty years of combat. He had failed Fiona. He rotated his hands, twisting the links of the chains that held him. He bent them back and forth. They had taken his weapon, so he would need all his training to get out of this situation. Even if he didn't survive, Fiona must live.

"From what I understand you're quite a legend where you come from." The Colonel's words echoed in the hollow steel building. "Why don't you make this easy and tell us where the rest of your men are."

"If that coward Eames told you who I was, then he must have explained that I will not talk."

"He did mention that they had tried to persuade you before." The Colonel paced around Eames. "The Captain is a wise man, though. Once he started talking, he couldn't stop. Perhaps you should reconsider. You're not on your homeland anymore."

Ardal lifted his head and gave the man a blank stare. He was mistaken if he thought intimidation would work. He was prepared to die. Death was a Hunter's reward. All he cared about was Fiona's safety. If he had to die to ensure that, then so be it.

A Hunter never divulged information.

Fiona shifted in the chair beside him. He glanced at her and saw her pain and fear. He should have killed Eames when he had the chance, but there was no room for regret. There was only one direction for a Hunter; forward, not backward.

"Let the woman go."

"I think not." The Major spoke this time. His voice was almost apologetic. "She knows too much. At the very least we'd have to guarantee that she didn't talk before we free her."

Ardal glanced at the man. He was a weakling and obviously unused to combat. "It would be a mistake."

The Major shook his head. "I have my orders."

"Where are the orders coming from?" Fiona's voice rose in anger. "Are you sure the government knows about this, or are you intelligence guys running things now?"

"We do what is best for the country." The Major crossed his arms. "You should have called the police when you found the wreckage."

"Why?" Fiona shook her head. "You would have done exactly what you're doing now."

"You've wasted our time."

Fiona motioned toward Captain Eames. "After your interrogation, you must know that they mean us no harm."

"I wouldn't be so sure." Colonel White brought a chair up to Fiona and sat down. "They have superior technological advances and they're at war. What's to prevent them from trying to conquer our planet?"

"That's utter nonsense." Fiona shook her head. "It was a crash, for goodness sake. They had injured and dead."

"According to Captain Eamon, these are vicious rebels who were slated for execution. They overpowered his crew, killing hundreds with their bare hands. They caused the vessel to crash. Surely you can see that we can't have creatures like that living on our planet. They must be hunted and destroyed like the animals they are."

Ardal sensed Fiona's revulsion. He should have been prepared for it. She was too gentle a soul to understand the ways of Hunters and combat. It was a couple of seconds before he realized that her disgust was not with him. She was repulsed by what her people intended to do to his men. His bond increased tenfold in that moment and he sent a surge of love toward her.

She swayed a bit under the onslaught, but at least her shock was gone. In its place he had sent her hope, belief that she would survive, and confidence that she would escape. Her compassion and faith in him made it possible. He would not fail her.

"You're not getting away with this." Fiona straightened her shoulders.

The Colonel chuckled and stood. "We've been getting away with it for decades. You don't honestly believe these are the first aliens to land on our planet."

"But they've never harmed us."

"You don't know that." The Major leaned back against the table next to Eamon. "There are quite a few incidents that we can't explain away. If they didn't mean harm, they would approach us openly."

"And be killed for the effort." Ardal did not hide his contempt.

Did these men think Hunters were idiots? He might not have heard of this planet before yesterday, but he knew the type. He had seen plenty of primitive worlds in his thirty-five years. There was no reasoning with the inhabitants. They reacted out of fear. Fear of the unknown.

Fear of change.

Fear of growth.

It was all too common. It was not his job to explain, only to follow orders and win. He had seen too many battles in too many war zones to believe that peace was attainable. Peace meant sharing and there was always someone who thought their needs were greater and more justified than anyone else.

Only power was understood and respected.

Ardal straightened in his chair. The time for talking was past. He focused his mind connection and sent a warning to his men. They would continue without him if he died. He flexed his neck from side to side and lowered his heart rate. He glanced at Eamon and saw the man pale. It was good that the Captain knew his minutes of life were limited. A coward without honor was lucky to be put out of his misery.

"I see our visitor is getting restless." Major Thomas pushed away from the table. "It won't be long now. We're setting up a lab. We'll get the information we need."

"It will not work."

"Pain has a way of loosening the tongue." The Colonel's voice held a hint of anticipation.

"It is primitive." Ardal twisted his hands behind his back. The links of the chain were almost broken. "Only a weak man would be affected by it."

"Oh, we don't intend to use it on you." The Major walked over to Fiona. "I've found that even the strongest of people cannot bear to see others in pain."

"You speak of honor. Is there honor in allowing another to suffer?" White came close to Ardal. "I have to wonder at what kind of man would let a woman suffer for his sins."

Rage seared his body.

With a quick snap the handcuff was broken and Ardal had the Colonel by the throat. He squeezed his esophagus making it impossible for the man to breathe or speak. The Major rushed at him, but Ardal slammed the base of his hand up into his nose and then chopped his adam's apple. The Major slumped to his knees clawing at his throat before dying.

Captain Wilson grabbed Fiona and used her to shield himself.

Ardal snapped the Colonel's neck and threw him down. "Hiding behind a woman holds no honor."

"Guard," Wilson yelled.

Wilson backed away with Fiona firmly in front of him. He was headed toward the door. "The MP's will be here within seconds."

Ardal kept pace with them. He glanced down at Wilson's knee and back up to Fiona. She looked at him for a second and then she acted. She heaved back her foot and booted the man's leg. He stumbled, but before he could recover Ardal had his hands around his throat. His neck was broken before Fiona could move away.

Ardal pulled her close.

He could hear men running in their direction. He had to make Fiona safe. He grabbed Wilson's weapon from his side before taking the other two men's guns. He handed one to Fiona.

"Do you know how to use this?"

She nodded before explaining.

She held it away from her. "Release the safety." She pushed a button in.

"Cock it." She pulled back on the upper end of it.

"The trigger releases the bullet." She put her finger on a curved area.

"All you need to do is point and shoot."

Ardal shoved one of the guns in his waistband before following Fiona's instructions. Primitive it might be, but as long as it stopped the men, he was not going to complain.

"You can't leave me here." Eamon's voice was a low whine. "They've threatened to dissect me."

Ardal turned and pointed the weapon. One shot and the Captain was out of his misery. Fiona's gasp concerned him, but there was no time to deal with her wishes right now. Her safety was all that mattered and as long as these men lived, she would not be safe.

"Come."

He grabbed her hand and headed toward the rear door. They reached it just as the first soldier entered the building. Ardal shot him and then pulled Fiona outside. It was a large camp, with at least twenty buildings. Men were streaming out of only three, though. Ardal pushed Fiona behind him and started toward the first group.

He raised his gun, but before he had a chance to fire, there was large roaring from the sky. Dust and gravel were twisted and blown into their faces.

It was another helicopter.

Ardal pushed closer to the steel building, ensuring that Fiona was completely covered by his body. He moved to aim for the incoming aircraft, but its weapons started spitting bullets all around. Within seconds the first wave of soldiers were lying on the ground.

A surge of mind connection hit him like a brick to the head. It was crude but effective. *We've come to help.* Ardal acknowledged the message. He had no idea who these people were, but their thoughts felt like Hunters. He stayed in place, keeping Fiona behind him. He could not trust these new warriors. It might be a trick to lull him into letting his guard down. If so they would be disappointed. A Hunter never relaxed his guard.

Another wave of soldiers was gunned down before the helicopter landed. Once on the ground, six men jumped out with weapons and spread out in a circle. Ardal kept Fiona behind him as he moved to the aircraft. The newcomers shot any soldier who obstructed his path. He felt Fiona's fear. He blocked it as he focused on their escape. By the time he reached the helicopter, there were no other soldiers standing.

The men who had come to their rescue were now checking all of the buildings. There was the odd report of a bullet being fired, but other than the helicopter blades, the area was quiet. The bodies of at least fifty soldiers littered the ground. Ardal waited with his weapons ready. One by one the newcomers walked back to the aircraft, their guns lowered as they approached.

All six of them stopped in front of Ardal. They looked to be in their late twenties, dark hair and dark eyes. There was coldness in those eyes, though. One of the men raised his gun at Fiona. Ardal pushed her behind him and aimed his weapon for the kill.

"Who are you?"

The man with the gun lowered his arm. "I'd say a thank you was in order. We just saved your butt. The human needs to die. She is too dangerous as a witness."

"No." Ardal kept his weapon aimed. "She is with me."

One of the other men moved his hands as if to surrender, but a weapon dropped down his sleeve. He whipped it up and pointed it at Ardal's head.

Ardal was quicker.

He grabbed the arm holding the gun and bent it so the pistol was pointing at his attacker. His other hand still had its weapon pointed at the first man.

"I am Ardal, elite Hunter and last of the clan Rioge. One move and both of these men are dead." Ardal let his gaze focus on each man. "Who are you?"

The men lowered their weapons, but Ardal continued to hold his captive. Fiona was still hidden behind him and he could feel her body trembling. By Cygnus and Warrior, he would rather kill these men than have her upset.

"Answer."

"Are you really of the clan Rioge?" the man Ardal was holding asked. His voice held a hint of awe. "We've never met a leader before."

"So far all you have done is anger one." Ardal loosened his hold slightly. "How long have you been here?"

"Thirty years."

"Impossible." Ardal tightened his hold on his captive.

"This atmosphere changes our metabolism." The man grabbed at Ardal's hand. "We crashed here when we were children. Some of our instructors lived, but most died. We have been here ever since."

The planet had strengthened him, but to age slower seemed crazy. He searched each of the men's eyes and mind and found no subterfuge. There was sadness, loneliness, and ruthlessness, but no deception.

"The woman is to be left unharmed."

"That is dangerous." The man who had first threatened Fiona took a step forward.

"A true Hunter follows the Sacred Code and does not kill women or children."

"She is from earth." The man motioned to the bodies around him. "They kill Hunters on this planet."

"She is not the same." Ardal's voice was a growl. "I need your word as a Hunter and your allegiance to the Sacred Code that you will obey my order and protect her."

Ardal waited as each man gave his vow and then he released the man he was holding. The man gave him a grin and rubbed his neck. "You are truly strong."

Ardal grunted. "Too many years fighting and training. Did you have a plan when you came here?"

"We go by the seat of our pants." The man held out his hand. "I'm Catal. We're all from the clan Saidir."

Ardal shook his hand. "You use the customs of this planet."

"It is all we've known." Catal pointed to the other men. "This is Gur, Kerm, Turlo, Ern, and Lorcan our leader."

Ardal moved aside so that Fiona could come out from behind him. The men's eyes widened when they saw her. There was no doubt that she was beautiful, even by this planet's standards. That is not what Ardal saw though. She had a kind and giving soul that had accepted his men without question.

"Are you sure you can rely on her." Lorcan's voice was doubtful. "Women are seldom what they seem."

"I've dealt with the Kaladin and the Holman." Ardal raised an eyebrow. "This is not the first woman I have met."

"True, but you are secluded from them."

"That does not mean that I am ignorant of their ways."

Ardal looked down at Fiona who was shifting from foot to foot. These men made her nervous. It was a risk to trust them, but one he had to take. They were Hunters like him. He had made his own men aware of the new developments and they were concerned. They had wanted to send in a recovery team, but he had stopped it. They must not linger, though.

"We need to leave."

"We'll take the helicopter. Climb onboard."

Fiona hesitated. Ardal sensed her fear. "Where are we going?"

"We have a hidden spot about an hour away. The military has yet to find it."

"We were headed south." Fiona's voice sounded hoarse.

"It's only a slight detour." Kern held out his hand for her.

Fiona took the help and climbed aboard. Ardal followed and sat beside her. She fidgeted with her hands and he clasped them together in his. The other men were already seated and looked at Ardal's actions with raised eyebrows. He ignored them and pulled her close to his body. She sighed and leaned her head on his chest.

They landed in a thickly wooded area that had a small landing pad for the helicopter. Dense forest was on one side and on the other was a lake of clear, blue water. It was a paradise. The only thing ruining the image was the military equipment and weapons.

Ardal sent the direction and mileage they had covered to his men before climbing down from the chopper. Then he helped Fiona. They pulled a netting cover over the aircraft and then headed to a building that was partially covered by the trees.

Once inside Ardal could see that this was more than a temporary headquarters. There were maps, electronic equipment, and along one wall, floor to ceiling weapons on shelves. These men were serious about protecting themselves.

Now was the time for explanations. Ardal pulled out a chair and let Fiona sit. He then turned to the men who were taking seats around a large table. He cleared his throat.

"How did you know where to find us?"

"Chatter." Lorcan started taking off his gun belt. "The military was hot on the trail of someone."

"Did you guys really take apart a group of FD Warriors outside Timmins?" Catal put his elbows on the table and leaned toward Ardal.

"They were offensive." Ardal shrugged. "They attacked first."

"What happened to them?"

"They are dead."

"Not a wise move when you're trying to blend in." Lorcan sat. "I'm assuming that's what you're doing. The radar suggested that your ship crashed."

"It did." Ardal stood beside the table. "We were being sent here for execution. All Hunters are dead, except us."

The men around the table looked at him with blank expressions before glancing back at Lorcan. "Why would they do that? If memory serves me correctly, Hunters have always been needed to win the battles the Kaladin and their mates were too squeamish to fight."

"The Kaladin are no more. The high council is in hiding and the Holman have taken over the planet." Ardal clenched his hands. "They did not trust us to fight for them so they ordered us killed. All Hunters obeyed. My men and I were on a mission when the others were executed. Upon our return, we were herded unto the craft and flown to this planet to be jettisoned into space."

"You are alive, though." Catal eyes glittered with curiosity. "What happened?"

"I refused to obey." Ardal straightened away from the table. "My men deserved to die with honor."

Lorcan frowned. "Why were you sent here?"

"I have no idea." Ardal crossed his arms across his chest. "You have been here many years. Perhaps you know why."

Lorcan shrugged. "Not a clue."

"Why were you here?"

"Our teachers said it was necessary for training and research. I think they wanted to see how we reacted in a different atmosphere. After the crash, we scattered around this planet."

Kerm cleared his throat. "The teachers thought we'd be rescued. When that didn't happen they became involved in speeding up the technology on this planet in the hopes of being able to get home."

"Obviously they failed." Lorcan's voice was sarcastic. "We learned to survive on our own. We do quite well for being strangers."

"Have none of you married and had children?" Fiona's question seemed to shock them.

"We are Hunters." Lorcan's voice was harsh. "Besides, why would we want to take a mate from this godforsaken planet?"

"How lonely." Her voice was full of sadness.

Ardal agreed. His reason was because they had been denied a brotherhood. Cut off from their home and other Hunters would have been difficult. As children, they would not have been provided with the skills or training to survive. Yet, they had. The question was how and at what price.

Lorcan shrugged. "We have never had the desire so it's never been a problem."

Ardal frowned. There could only be one answer. "Do you still have your implants?"

"What implants?" The man called Kerm tilted his head.

"Hold out your arm." Ardal felt along the forearm and found the telltale bump. "You have them. Do you have any unusual skills?"

"Besides not aging?" The men all laughed. "No."

The implants were put in after birth. If they were active, then the Kaladin had always known where the boys were. The crash may have interrupted the signal. The military had taken his scanner so he had no way to check if they were active. Either way, it would be best to have them removed.

"If they are deactivated, they may still be used for tracking." Ardal looked at Fiona. "Can you remove them?"

She nodded. "Do you have any medical equipment or a first aid kit?"

Lorcan got up and searched through a cupboard before throwing a small plastic container at Fiona. She rummaged through it and found a small scalpel and bandages. She arranged the materials and disinfected her tools. When she was done, she glanced at Lorcan.

"You should go first. It will only take a few minutes."

"You can't be serious." Lorcan pushed away from the table. "I don't trust you."

Ardal reached out for the knife and then pointed at Kerm. "Come." The man held his arm out and Ardal made short work of removing the implant. Fiona put on the antibiotic cream and bandage. The rest of the men followed with Lorcan being the last. Then Ardal took a hammer to the implants, beating them until they were broken apart.

"These need to be burned, melted down, and buried. The Kaladin and Holman have known your location since you crashed." Ardal threw the hammer on the table. "They were coming here not only to execute us, but to track and kill you. That explains the size of the crew that was onboard."

"You mean they left us here all these years?"

"You were expendable." It was the reality of being a soldier. You were a pawn in another's game of power. "You became a problem when they decided that all Hunter blood was to be destroyed. They could not risk that you would one day come back to Cygnus and demand recognition as Hunters."

Lorcan pushed his chair away from the table. "We were children. Do you know what happened to those of us who were captured?"

Fiona shuddered. "Probably what they threatened to do to us."

Lorcan leaned toward her, his face screwed up with anger. "They ran them down like animals, and once they were caught they pulled them apart like laboratory rats. They had no mercy."

"I'm sorry." Fiona's voice shook.

Lorcan slammed his fist down on the table. "You people are monsters. Don't try and placate me with words. I will see you dead before I let you leave here alive."

Ardal snapped.

He picked Lorcan up and threw him against the wall. The man tried to stand, but collapsed on his stomach. Gur, Kerm, and Turlo rushed him next and he dealt with them in the same manner. Catal reached for a gun. Ardal pulled Ern close with a neck hold and used him as a shield.

He pushed Fiona behind him.

"You have no honor." He walked toward Catal with slow, steady steps. "You gave me your oath as a Hunter that she would not be harmed."

Catal used both hands to steady the gun. "I wasn't going to harm her."

"Then why defend Lorcan."

"He is the leader."

"No man can be a leader without honor." Ardal was now a foot away from Catal. He grabbed the gun and threw it down. "There should not be war among Hunters. We have seen enough of it because of the orders of others. Hunters do not kill each other."

Catal took a shaky breath and then sagged against the table. "I didn't know that rule."

"I do not think any of you know the Sacred Code." Ardal pushed Ern away. "It is not your fault, but if you refuse to live by the Sacred Code then I cannot treat you as Hunters. Understood?"

Catal nodded.

Ardal took a deep breath and eased his heart rate to slow the adrenaline coursing through his body. He would not make the mistake of trusting these men, for they were more men than Hunters. The blood ran true, but without the training and honor, they were no better than the Holman. He felt Fiona's fear and he wanted to destroy these men, but he would give them another chance. They had resources and knowledge that would be valuable to his men.

"How have you survived this long?" Ardal's voice was low.

"We hunt as our blood dictates." Ern rubbed his neck where Ardal had grabbed him.

"Who gives the orders?"

"We solicit orders." Lorcan heaved himself into a sitting position. "Humans are technologically behind and even the teachers couldn't bring them to a point where it would be possible for us to leave, so we learned to survive. We thrive by being Hunters and giving the humans what they want."

Fiona shivered behind him and a sense of foreboding skipped through his body. He looked back at her, touching her hair to comfort. She leaned into his hand and sighed. She was still afraid, but there was also great sadness in her.

"Who do these orders come from?" Ardal turned back to Lorcan, but kept his hand on Fiona. The touch of her was soothing.

"Humans bring us the orders. In the past it was in person, but now it is done through the Internet." Lorcan's voice was full of pride. "We fill a need and at the same time get to hunt. We get paid good money to do it."

Ardal's stomach tensed. "What do you hunt?"

"The enemy." Lorcan's voice was full of disdain. "We hunt humans.

Chapter 16

"You're assassins and mercenaries." She had known the truth before they had said it. The equipment in the building was the first clue. Then there was the helicopter. They needed a lot of money to outfit a place like this. It looked as if they could wage a war at a moment's notice.

"Explain." Ardal's voice was cold as steel.

"They kill for money." Fiona motioned around the room. "And from the looks of this stuff, they get paid a lot."

"You're not just a pretty face." Lorcan smirked. "It's amazing how many people want their loved ones, or enemies killed. They just don't want to do the dirty work. And we're real good at it."

"A Hunter does not get pleasure from killing. It is necessary, but never joyful."

"Is that another one of those codes we've never heard about?" Lorcan laughed. "You're full of one liners."

"You are ignorant of our ways." Ardal straightened his shoulders. "I have trained many a young Hunter and I will endeavor to help you."

"We are not children."

"True." Ardal's voice held regret. "I cannot undo what has happened to you, but I can help you obtain the honor and knowledge of a Hunter."

"We saved your butt back there." Lorcan pointed a finger at Ardal. "We don't need to hear a lecture from you about our behavior. If you hadn't been dragging this woman around, you probably wouldn't have been caught."

"A Hunter lives by two codes; those of the Warrior and those of the Sacred Code of the Hunter." Ardal looked at the other men in the room. "The first rule of the Sacred Code is that a Hunter does not betray his word."

Lorcan rolled his eyes. "That only happens in a perfect world."

"The first rule of the Warrior Code is that it is forbidden to kill or harm a woman or child." Ardal paused and looked at each man individually. "You have broken both of these codes. Another Hunter would not hesitate to kill you."

"You couldn't get within two yards of us if we didn't want you to." Lorcan's face was distorted with anger.

"Your words show ignorance and your actions tell me you have no wish to change."

"Why should I want to?" Lorcan started to walk toward Ardal. "Who are you to try and change us?"

Fiona sensed trouble. Ardal reached for her and again she found herself staring at his back. He took this protection stuff a little too seriously, but a part of her knew that it went deeper than that. Their bond meant that he would suffer if anything happened to her.

"I am your leader."

"You expect us to follow you because you're clan Rioge?" Lorcan snorted. "I could kill you now."

"You live by violence." Ardal's voice was sad. "A true Hunter lives by honor."

"We did what was necessary." Lorcan pulled a knife from his belt. "I've heard enough of your words."

Catal stepped forward and put his hand on Lorcan's arm. "We don't want a fight. We have done our best to survive on this planet."

"Now you know differently." Ardal shook his head. "My wish is that we work together, but together as Hunters."

"You oppose us." Lorcan shook off Catal's restraint and threw down his knife. "We should have left you to die."

"We do not have to be enemies. All Hunters belong to the brotherhood." Ardal's tone was conciliatory. "You are badly trained and let anger influence you."

Fiona stepped from around Ardal. "They have lived in hiding for too long. The stress can make you do stupid things."

Kerm nodded. "Lorcan, I can't believe you would consider attacking a Hunter of the clan Rioge."

"Do you wish to be true Hunters?" Ardal straightened his shoulders. "I am prepared to train you, but I understand if you believe you are too old. You look to be as old as my youngest soldier, but your years are many more."

Ardal looked at each of the men and waited for them to show their agreement. Fiona held her breath and waited. These men would have to accept Ardal's command and a commitment to a new way of living. A life ruled by honor. Ardal waited for the nod of agreement from each man before straightening his shoulders.

He walked over to Lorcan and lifted his head. "Do you accept?"

The man nodded. "I'm not a fool. You're definitely of the clan Rioge. Our teachers tried to explain the difference between the clans, but there's nothing like firsthand experience."

Ardal gripped the man's shoulder. "You have learned the first lesson. Know your commander."

"We have others of us who should be consulted about our decision. They can also provide interference." Catal's voice was low and he glanced at Fiona for a second before his eyes skittered away. "We don't want the humans finding us."

"Then arrange it." Ardal looked back at her and smiled. "We need to leave. The rest of my men are awaiting us in Toronto."

"We'll ready the helicopter." Catal motioned for the others to follow him.

When they were alone Fiona cleared her throat. "What happened here?"

"These men are still like children at the beginning of their training." Ardal shook his head. "Their wounds may be too deep to heal."

Fiona looked up at him. His dark eyes held a sadness that she had not seen before. "Because they were abandoned on earth?"

"It is more than that. They had no direction or brothers." Ardal reached for her hands. "A Hunter is not a man alone. He is one with his brothers. Always he has others with him to guide and direct."

"What about you?" Fiona leaned her head on his chest. "You are in command. Who guides you?"

"I have always had others of my clan, but now there is only me." He sighed and rubbed his chin against her head. "Perhaps that is why I have been given the gift of a pair bond."

"So I'm a consolation prize?" Fiona grinned and looked up at him. "You've got bad luck."

"No."

Ardal's voice was serious. The world disappeared as he gazed into her eyes and she couldn't look away. There was a fire and the promise of forever in his eyes. A sense of destiny and fate came into play as he lowered his head to her. The touch of his mouth sent a shiver of desire through her body.

His caress was a bolt of lightning to her soul, awakening every cell within her body. His tongue traced the outline of her lips. She quivered and sighed with the perfection of the moment, opening herself to his searching.

He didn't disappoint. He explored and tantalized. He brought her closer, tightening and caressing her back and arms as he plundered her mouth. The friction of his tongue against hers sent shivers of delight throughout her body. Her arms wrapped around his neck and she held him close, allowing her own hunger to fire the melding of their lips. Her tongue dueled with his in a slow, seductive play. She gave to him without fear and from somewhere deep within her, she recognized her true mate; the other half of herself.

How long they kissed she didn't know, but it had felt like mere seconds of ecstasy. He pulled away and she moaned her regret. He rested his forehead against hers and exhaled a deep breath. His body trembled and she was surprised that she could cause such a reaction. Ardal was a man who faced death without flinching, but a kiss seemed to affect him as deeply as it did her.

"I do not regret touching you." He kissed her nose and then leaned back. "I will always remember the pleasure and delight of holding you in my arms. If you should decide that you do not want me as a mate, then I will live with this memory forever."

"A man like you wouldn't be lonely for long." Fiona tried to keep her voice light.

"No." Ardal shook his head. "Fate has chosen you. I could not be with another."

"Never?" Fiona's voice was a hoarse whisper.

"There is only one for a Hunter once he has been bonded."

"Humans can change their partners."

"It is good that you have choices."

"So do you."

"Having tasted you I could never want another." Ardal's gaze did not leave her face. "I never expected to bond so there is no need for you to be sad."

"It doesn't seem fair." Fiona twisted a strand of her hair in her finger.

"It is the way of a Hunter. Life does not have to be fair to be lived."

At some level she couldn't disagree with him. It hadn't been fair that David had become obsessed with her. There was nothing that made sense in the fact that she had to run away from her friends and family just to stay alive. There was no justice in the fact that the law protected David's rights, but not hers. There really was no point in wishing for something that wasn't possible.

With a sigh she walked to the window. The other men had not returned. She started tapping her fingers on the window sill. A sense of unease knotted her stomach. They had stayed here too long. She knew it was a reaction from the past year on the run, but she'd learned the hard way to follow her instincts.

David had always been clever. He'd fooled her family and friends and even the other interns. They'd thought he was the most sincere and caring doctor on the staff. The first time she'd tried to tell a fellow intern of the horror David had made of her life, she'd laughed and accused her of possessiveness.

She'd honestly thought Fiona was jealous because a nurse had been bragging about dating David. Fiona didn't want David. As far as she was concerned if he found another victim then she'd be safe, but her conscience wouldn't let her walk away without warning David's next victim.

When David learned about her confiding to another, he'd beaten her so severely that she'd been hospitalized. He'd threatened to kill her family if she said anything, so she'd lied to the police. She'd told them she'd been in the wrong section of town and hadn't paid attention.

When she'd left the hospital, he was waiting for her. He'd brought along her sister and that's when she knew he'd never let her go free. She'd made plans to leave that night and within a week her life on the run had begun.

As far as David and her family were concerned, she'd died the day she left. She'd disappeared without a trace. For all intents and purposes she was dead. The thought of David finding her was worse than being captured again by the military.

"It will not happen." Ardal was behind her, his voice firm and sincere. "I will protect you."

"There are some things you can't promise." Fiona leaned back into him.

Ardal squeezed her shoulders, his touch comforting. "I can see why Lorcan feels this world is unworthy. Men do not hurt women on Cygnus."

"Then you are more evolved than us." Fiona sighed. "Not all men are bad. My father is a good man. Maybe that's why I was so naïve and trusting. I'd never come across someone like David before."

"You will not have to face him again."

"I never thought I would be able to trust another man. It feels wonderful to be with you." Fiona turned to face Ardal. "It's the killing I can't deal with. I don't know if I'll ever be able to accept it."

"It is the life of a Hunter. I cannot…" Whatever he was going to say was loss in the loud alarm that shrilled throughout the cabin.

Fiona's heart started to race. She turned to leave by the door, but Ardal stopped her. He pushed her behind him. He didn't have long to wait. The door flung open and Catal was thrown inside. The rest of the men followed, landing in a heap in the center of the cabin.

Ardal flexed his neck from side to side. The next seconds seemed like an eternity. Fiona held her breath, waiting for the inevitable strike.

She was not disappointed.

The first man through the door was thrown against the wall.

The second yelled; his voice low and familiar. "It is Firbin."

Ardal relaxed his muscles and turned to face Jehon on the floor. He went to him and offered his assistance, but Jehon brushed him aside and stood.

"Where is the alarm?" Jehon kicked at Erm.

Erm pointed to a button on the wall and Jehon punched it. Silence finally. Any louder and her eardrums would have exploded. She sagged back against the wall and watched the men on the floor sit up. They looked surprised and defeated.

"You disobeyed." Ardal's disapproval was almost a living entity.

"We could not warn you." Jehon motioned to the men on the floor. "We were unsure if they had a means of hearing."

"They have enough surveillance equipment." Fiona moved from the wall. "You scared me half to death."

"Our apologies." Firbin gave her a grin. "You were never in danger, though."

"But you were." Ardal moved to the young man. "Insubordination will not be tolerated."

"No sir." Firbin hung his head. "We regretted leaving you alone, especially when we knew that you had been captured. We were only a short distance from this place."

"You would have done the same for us." Jehon walked over to the wall of weapons. "We will have to learn to use these primitive instruments."

"Primitive, but effective." Ardal's voice was dry. "These men you have disposed of so easily were our rescuers. Their weapons kill as well as ours."

Jehon turned to the men who were getting up from the floor. He raised his eyebrow. "We were not certain that they would leave you unharmed."

"You do not trust your commander's ability."

Fiona bit back her smile. Ardal's words were innocent enough, but the tone of voice gave him away. One glance at Jehon and she knew he wasn't fooled by it either. He just shook his head.

"You are a leader amongst leaders." Jehon's tone was as dry as Ardal's. "Why else would you have been chosen the personal protector of the high council?"

"But to earn your respect would be something." Ardal pointed to the men and introduced them.

"You two know each other too well." Fiona rubbed her arms and looked out the window.

"We have fought together since we were boys in training." Ardal nodded to Catal. "How long to learn these weapons.?"

Catal shrugged. "They are easy."

"Show Jehon. His gift is machines."

Catal gave Ardal a searching glance of respect and then went to Jehon. He pulled down a machine gun and let Jehon feel its weight.

Ardal then turned to Lorcan. "How can we leave this place?"

Lorcan rubbed his neck. "I would suggest the helicopter as the fastest, but it won't take all of us."

Ardal nodded and looked at Firbin. "How did you arrive?"

"We hiked through the forest. It took about an hour."

"Kerm, Catal, and Ern will come with us to Toronto." Ardal gave Lorcan a stern glance. "Will you be safe here?"

"They don't know about this place."

"That was before you took apart their base." Ardal crossed his arms. "If I were in command that would not be left unresolved. I would not rest until I was certain that the perpetrators were dead."

"But you aren't from this planet." Lorcan rolled his eyes. "They will try, but we are better."

"Your cockiness will be your undoing." Ardal glanced at Jehon. "My men had no problem dealing with you."

Lorcan pursed his lips. "You are trained Hunters. The men of this planet do not have the same skills."

"I trust you know what you speak of." Ardal's eyes narrowed. "They will not be so unprepared next time."

"We've been doing this for over thirty years." Lorcan's voice was defensive. "We can run circles around them."

"Now they know that there are more than one group of Hunters on this planet, though."

"We have not fought the military directly before." Lorcan glanced at Fiona. "It isn't wise to discuss this in front of her. If she is captured she will talk."

Firbin stiffened at Fiona's side. He made a move toward Lorcan, but Ardal's stopped him with a shake of his head. Fiona held her breath. Lorcan may have accepted Ardal, but she wasn't one of them. It was understandable that he might suspect her of taking sides against them.

"I wouldn't want anyone to be captured." Fiona shivered with remembered horror at what the Colonel had threatened. "I was trained as a doctor. I've taken an oath to save people, not hurt them."

Lorcan crossed his arms. "You're one of them and a woman. You can't be trusted."

Jehon snapped the gun he was holding at Lorcan. "You disrespect a woman?"

Ardal held up his arms. "Lorcan and the others crashed on this planet when they were children. Their training is not complete."

Jehon lowered his weapon. "I do not have patience with children. We are warriors not teachers."

"That is why I command. They are soldiers, but one day they will be Hunters." Ardal's voice was calm. "They have given me their vow that they will accept my command and not harm Fiona."

"It makes no sense to take on the burden of the woman." Lorcan kept his voice reasonable. "If you're trying to escape then leave her here. Once you're safe, you can send for her."

"She helped us at great risk to herself." Firbin's voice was firm. "We would not leave her to fight alone."

"We'll take care of her."

"No." Ardal's voice boomed. "She stays with me."

Confusion flitted across Lorcan's face. He glanced at her and then back at Ardal. "What's going on here?"

Ardal sighed. "You are under my command now. It is only right that you should know."

Firbin moved in front of her and Jehon's hold on the gun tightened. Whatever they expected Ardal to announce they thought protection was necessary. Crazy as it seemed, they were preparing to fight again. When would it end?

"I have bonded to Fiona."

Lorcan's confusion changed to incredulity. He grabbed a gun from the table and pointed it at Fiona. "That's impossible."

Chapter 17

"You cannot kill her." Ardal forced Lorcan's arm up just as he fired a shot. "Even as children, Hunters understand the pair bond."

Catal's voice broke the silence. "It's a legend. There is no truth in it."

"That is what we thought." Ardal watched Fiona leave the cabin with Firbin. He sensed her unease over the Hunter ways, but there was nothing he could do to change. A Hunter lived by the code, no matter what.

"Our implants were deactivated when we were on Cygnus." Jehon spoke now. "Any protection, enhancement, or control over our bodies has been turned off for several months."

"So the implants prevented you from mating."

"It would seem so." Ardal shook his head. "There is no understanding the connection because it was considered a myth. No Hunter has been faced with this situation."

"But you accept that it is bonding?" Lorcan snorted. "It could just be plain old lust. I mean she is a gorgeous woman, even by earth's standards."

Ardal's eyes narrowed. The urge to hit the man was great. He was a mere child in terms of training, though. He stilled his breathing and heart rate. He would not react in anger.

"I feel what she feels. I know her thoughts." Ardal paused and then said in an even lower voice. "We have not mated, but I have no desire for another. I will not leave her."

"How many others have you tried?" Lorcan sputtered. "The Kaladin withheld a great joy from us."

"It is understandable." Ardal motioned to the closed cabin door. "I sense her at all times. She is a part of me. Only a well-trained Hunter would be able to control that and still be a warrior."

"Have you never felt the urge to bond?" Jehon's question forced the men to look at him. "If your implants were deactivated, then this could have happened to you too."

"We have been around women on this planet, but not in the sense you're talking about. They are the enemy." Kerm took a step closer to Ardal. "Is it possible that this hasn't happened because we did not believe it?"

Ardal shrugged. "I knew immediately that there was something different about how I felt. I never believed in the legends either, but I know Fiona is the other half to me."

"So she has to stay with you?" Kerm seemed to be struggling with this information.

"It is the only way I can keep her safe."

"And you're content with this?"

"I gave her my vow."

Lorcan threw his hands up in the air. "A woman like that is bound to draw attention. You can't walk anywhere and not stand out."

"We have noticed." Ardal's tone was dry. "I am not stupid. All I know is that we are connected."

"So you want us to continue as if nothing has happened."

"You said you were monitoring this planet's communications. Then remain doing so."

"And let you guys have all the fun?" Lorcan gave a dry laugh. "Don't we have a choice?"

It was Jehon who answered. "No."

Lorcan gave him a long look and then nodded. "You're right, of course. We'll contact you if we notice a problem."

"I trust you to protect yourselves. If there is a problem, then you are to join us." Ardal was uneasy about leaving these men alone, but what choice did he have? "We will need to know how things work on this planet. Do we have time for that?"

"No. If you're going to Toronto you can't take the helicopter." Lorcan went to one of the maps on the wall. "Toronto is here and it's very populated. To land there secretly is impossible. We usually take road or train transportation."

"There will be seven of us."

"Take the boat across the lake. We keep an emergency vehicle there. It holds seven."

Ardal looked at the map. They were further south than they had been when they'd taken the bus. They were still hours away from anonymity.

He had already heard from his other men. They'd all reached their destination without incident. It was only his group that had garnered any interest. He didn't like being the decoy because Fiona was with them, but he was relieved that his men were safe.

"Fiona says that we need to use money so the authorities cannot trace us."

"Absolutely." Lorcan pulled a picture off the wall and exposed a metal box. He twisted the numbered circle and opened the door. He pulled out a stack of bills. "This should keep you safe for a while."

"Thank you." Ardal grasped Lorcan's shoulder. "The second rule of the code is a Hunter always helps his brother."

"That's why we've survived." Lorcan smiled. "Finally, we'll have others of the brotherhood with us."

"Hunters true and right. We are honored you are with us." Ardal nodded toward the men who would be accompanying them then looked back to Lorcan. "Tell the rest of the brotherhood on this planet that their implants must be removed. Even if they are deactivated, they can still be used for tracking. Warn them of the Holman dangers."

"I'll do it immediately. We cannot afford to lose any more brothers."

"By Cygnus and Warrior we will meet again."

Fiona yawned and sat up. Ardal grunted as she pushed away from him. Stretching her arms above her head she smiled back at him. The man made her happy. There was no getting around that fact. As frightened as she'd been in the past, Ardal and his men made her feel safe.

She wasn't kidding herself, though. She didn't approve of the killing. She doubted that she would ever be able to accept it. She wasn't fool enough to think love could change a person. Ardal had been a Hunter too long to know anything else. There was also the problem of him being from another planet.

"Where are we now?"

"We're just entering the city." Catal spoke from the front. He turned, but his eyes shied away from looking at her directly. "Soon we will begin to separate. Firbin and I are to go with you."

"We aren't staying together?" Fiona looked up at Ardal.

"It is safer." Ardal's voice was low. "They are looking for us. Lorcan has advised us that the police have sent out our descriptions."

"They can't know that for sure. You killed them all."

"They are claiming a terrorist cell attacked a military base. They want us in connection with the incident. It is dangerous for us to be together." Ardal put his hand on her shoulder. "I need to make sure that my men are situated and then I will come for you."

"No." Fear shook her insides. "I can't go back there. David will find me."

"Firbin and Catal will keep you safe."

"But I won't feel safe." Fiona's voice was a low whisper.

Ardal leaned close. "I am only a thought away. I will be in constant connection."

"It isn't the same." A stab of pain pierced her heart. What was wrong with her? One minute she was questioning whether she could accept his way of life and the next she couldn't live without him. Tears started to fill her eyes, but she brushed them away with an impatient fingers.

Ardal captured her hand and rubbed it against his cheek. "There is no need for fear. My men are the best."

"Promises are not always possible to keep." Fiona's chest tightened as she considered how much her life had changed in the past couple of days. Now the mere thought of letting Ardal out of her sight sent her into a panic. What if he didn't return?

Ardal gathered her close in his arms. His lips moved over her ears sending shivers of delight through her. "I will always be with you."

"Reading my mind again?"

"Even in death I will be at your side forever."

"Somehow that doesn't comfort me." Fiona pushed away from Ardal and wiped her eyes. "Okay, I'll go with Firbin and Catal."

Ardal held her gaze for several seconds before nodding his agreement. She had spent her whole life without a man. Surely a few days or weeks without Ardal wouldn't be that hard to take. She shivered as she thought about how near to David she would be. Perhaps she should contact the Woman's Underground Network and start another life.

A life on the run.

A life without Ardal.

He hugged her closer. She knew that he'd sensed or heard her thoughts and even though the pain of living without him was almost unbearable, she knew he'd let her go. Whatever her decision, it was hers to make.

Ardal would honor her choice.

"My men need me. We are strangers here and my duty is to ensure their safety. I will be with you as soon as possible."

She glanced up at him and smiled. Of course he needed to be with his men. He was the leader and he would never forsake them. A lesser man might think only of himself, but not Ardal.

That's why she loved him.

Ardal's muscles jerked tighter around her. He had heard and understood. With a sigh she pushed away and straightened her shoulders. She was strong. She had lived her life on her own before and that is what she intended to do now. Besides, she still had two strong Hunters who would protect her.

"So who gets dropped off first?"

"Catal has chosen a small hotel outside the northern end of the city. You will be the first to leave." Ardal cleared his throat. "We need the vehicle."

Fiona shrugged. "We can rent one, or there is public transit if necessary."

"Public transit?" Firbin raised an eyebrow. "Is that safe?"

"Not for you guys, but I can get away with it." Fiona rolled her eyes. "Women can change their looks easy with a hat, or a bottle of hair dye."

"No." Ardal's voice was commanding. "Your hair is not to be touched."

"It will grow out." Fiona pulled a clump of it forward. "It's too distinctive a color."

"It is something unseen on Cygnus." Ardal shook his head. "You will not change it."

Fiona looked at him for a few seconds. There was determination in his eyes and something else. A hopelessness, almost despair. Suddenly she knew it wasn't the color of her hair that mattered, but the fact she'd resort to lies to protect herself. He saw that as a failure to protect her.

"If you wish. There's no point in arguing over it." There was an audible gasp from the other Hunters. "Do men and women not disagree on your planet?

"No." Ardal's voice was firm. "A woman decides and a man does not challenge."

Nice to know. Fiona glanced at the other men and smiled. "On earth, men and women can discuss things together. They compromise so that both will be happy. You guys better get used to it if you want to blend in."

"What if we cannot change?"

"Then you'll look like wimps." Fiona pursed her lips. "Then again, that might not be a bad idea. No one would mistake you as anything but normal human men."

"That is true." Catal's voice was dry. "This is a planet of weak males. Women have made it impossible for men to be who they truly are. Their history tells the tales of great warriors, but no more. Women have softened them too much."

"It is not soft to abhor violence. Women give life. They want to ensure their children grow up to live in peace." Fiona crossed her arms. "What about the women who are still terrorized by men who show their power with their fist?"

Silence followed her words. Firbin clenched his hands beside her and she could see Jehon's frown in the rear view mirror. The other men were avoiding her eyes.

"What did I say wrong now?"

"On Cygnus it is women who decide the wars, and men who fight them." Ardal's voice was gentle. "As warriors we abhor the violence, but there is no choice. We keep our planet safe."

"Women do not have children on Cygnus." Firbin spoke now. He looked at Fiona with hooded eyes. "That has not happened for eons; almost as far back as when the Sacred Codes were written."

"Never?"

Firbin shook his head. "That would be risking a genetic mistake."

"Such as red hair?" Fiona shook her hair about her face.

She smiled at the shocked expressions on the men's faces. Had they never considered that some mistakes were good? It wasn't her place to criticize. These men came from a different culture. Just like earth, there were different cultures and attitudes that sometimes seemed unusual. As long as they didn't hurt women, she could live with it.

"Boy you guys are in for some surprises," Fiona nodded to a hotel where they had just pulled into. "This looks like it might do for a short-term stop."

Ardal nodded and Jehon started to slow the van down. They were parked at the hotel office within a couple of minutes. Catal jumped out and Firbin followed. When it was Fiona's turn, she looked up at Ardal. She longed to kiss him goodbye, but didn't want to make it difficult for him in front of his men.

His eyes turned molten and before she knew what he meant to do, his hand had clasped the back of her head. He pulled her close and captured her lips. It was searing, almost soul destroying in its intensity. He gave all of himself to her and she gave herself back. If something went wrong she would have this to remember.

"Go." His voice was hoarse as he released her.

She nodded and climbed from the van. She kept her back to him and waited until she heard the tires screech away before she dared to look at the retreating van. He was gone and so was her heart.

She rubbed her arms against the cool chill of the late summer night. "We'd better get ourselves a room."

"Two rooms." Firbin cleared his throat. "We will take turns standing guard outside your room."

"That's nuts." Fiona started for the office door. "I can sleep on one bed and if you insist on staying awake to keep guard, then you'll only need one bed for the two of you."

"It is forbidden for a Hunter to stay with a woman."

"We slept together in the cave. How is this different?"

"This is proper room."

"Sleeping is sleeping." Honestly these guys loved to argue over semantics. "Besides, you can't stand outside, you'll be too noticeable and they have cameras in the hallways."

"Ardal will be upset."

"He'll understand." Fiona opened the office door. "There's nothing to argue about. Let's get a room and then we can eat."

"This will not be like the other restaurant?" Firbin gave her a crooked smile.

Fiona shook her head. "You guys have quite the understated sense of humor."

Their room was on the third floor. The elevator was slow, and the halls stunk of stale alcohol. It was definitely not a five star hotel, but the possibility of anyone noticing or caring about their sleeping arrangements was slim. Fiona doubted anything would be considered shocking in this place.

She walked to the bathroom and flipped the light on. Small, but it had all the necessary items. There was even a toiletry package. A bath would have been nice, but not here. A shower would have to do.

"We should probably get some clean clothes tomorrow." Fiona leaned against the door and looked at the two men. They were standing at attention as if waiting her orders. "You can relax. Firbin, you know that."

He laughed and sat down in one of the chairs by the window. "I am still unsure of how to behave around you now that you are pair bonded to our leader."

Fiona shrugged. "Why should that make a difference?"

"Everything about this planet is new. " Firbin gestured to Catal. "Perhaps you could give me a quick lesson on how to behave."

"We don't try to fit in." Catal looked down at the floor. "Our experience of the people on earth hasn't been very warming."

"You have survived." Firbin's voice showed his interest. "You must understand the ways of the planet."

Catal looked up, his eyes hooded. "I'm afraid I'm just realizing how little I really know about humans. I thought I knew it all, but now I'm not so sure."

"What made you change your mind?" Fiona sat on the bed.

"You." Catal tilted his head. "I didn't think humans were capable of deep emotion. I believed that we were different and there was no mixing of the two."

"So you used us as you wanted? You hunted us as if we were no better than animals."

"Yes." Catal sighed. "Now I realize that it was my own people who deserve my disdain. They're the ones who left us out here to die and ordered all Hunters dead."

Fiona nodded. "You're still in shock. You need time to figure out what you believe."

"Time is something we have a lot of on this planet."

Firbin frowned. "I don't understand."

"We age slower here."

Fiona smiled. "Good thing Ardal is older than me." She stood and wrapped her hair in a scarf. "Let's go and eat. I'm starved."

There was a restaurant attached to the hotel and even though the meal was nothing spectacular, Fiona was thankful for the food. It had been hours since they'd eaten and she was finding it hard to think on an empty stomach. And thinking was something she needed to do.

By the time they got back to the room the three of them were on easier terms. Firbin was already comfortable with Fiona, but it took

Catal to the end of the meal to realize that she held no ill-will toward him. She felt sympathy for the man, especially when she remembered Ardal's words about being stranded without any connection with his own kind.

Fiona flopped down on the bed. She was exhausted. Travel and fear had taken their toll. All she wanted was a shower and bed.

"Do you guys mind if I commandeer the bathroom first?"

Firbin's eyes widened. "There is no need to ask. It is as you wish."

Catal laughed. "You have a lot to learn about humans. They are a selfish lot."

"I disagree." Fiona groaned as she pushed away from the bed. "I asked first. I didn't lock myself in there for a couple of hours."

"True." Catal shook his head. "You are a constant surprise."

"That's because you've never taken the time to understand the people of this planet." Fiona walked toward Catal who was standing near the window. "There are good, decent humans."

Then there was a knock at the door. Panic flooded Fiona.

They were found.

Chapter 18

She froze.

Firbin moved to the door. His hands were clenched and all expression had left his eyes. He was all Hunter, readying himself for the attack. Catal moved to the opposite side of the room and had pulled out a gun.

She had to do something before violence ripped through the room. She went to the door and spoke without opening it. "Who is it?"

"I was just in the restaurant." The voice was male and hesitant. "You left your bag on the chair."

Fiona released the breath she'd been holding and sagged against the door. She looked at Firbin and nodded her head, before opening the door. There was a young man in his mid-twenties standing there with her backpack in his hands. All her emergency information, money, and supplies were in that bag. The man was a lifesaver.

"Thank you," she said as she reached for the bag. "I'd be lost without this."

"I know you or your brothers would have noticed it eventually, but I didn't think it was wise to leave it to chance. I tried to catch you before you got to your room, but I wasn't fast enough."

Fiona opened the door wider, but still blocked the entrance. He looked pleasant enough, with blonde hair and blue eyes, but she wasn't about to trust anyone. Honest or not, the more people who saw them, the greater the risk they'd be identified.

"I appreciate it." Fiona tilted her head as she looked at him. "How did you know they were brothers?"

"You're kidding. The same skin tone, dark hair and eyes were a dead giveaway." He shrugged. "Besides they look alike. I just assumed you're related."

Fiona laughed. "Well, I never thought I looked like those two. Thanks for bringing me the bag."

When the door was closed and the danger passed Fiona turned back to the two Hunters. She frowned and studied them closer. They did look like brothers. There were some differences, but the similarities were striking. They looked a cross between Native American and Irish. Maybe they'd blend in just fine.

"He was honest." Fiona pushed away from the door. "And very observant."

"We are brothers." Firbin moved back to the chair.

"That's what Ardal said." Fiona shrugged. It wasn't a big deal, especially if they all came from a test tube. They were bound to have similar genes. "I'm going for a shower."

Two days later there was still no word from the other Hunters. Fiona was starting to go stir crazy. She wasn't allowed out of the room. Catal and Firbin took turns bringing food back. They thought her looks too distinctive and they couldn't risk her being recognized. There was only so much television a person could watch and not go crazy.

Firbin found the whole thing fascinating. He'd never seen shows that were strictly for entertainment. Hunters focused on training and skills development. Entertainment was for the rulers of their planet.

She was about ready to pull her hair out when Firbin suddenly stood and turned the television off. Catal glanced toward the door and straightened his shoulders. There was a knock and Firbin opened it.

Five Hunters walked into the room.

None of them was Ardal.

She only recognized Darrogh. The other men glanced at her and then looked away. Fiona's enthusiasm started to shrivel as she felt their disapproval. She sat and waited. She hid her smile as the others greeted Firbin. He was the youngest of their unit and they slapped him on the back in greeting.

"You have been lazy." Darrogh's voice boomed in the room. "Sitting around and doing nothing. Your leg should be healed by now."

"Fiona has cared for it." Firbin glanced at her with a grin. "She is a tough taskmaster."

"Ah." Darrogh raised an eyebrow. "She is a woman. They have no place with Hunters."

Firbin's eyes widened. He glanced at the other men who stood immobile. "You are mistaken. She has been a great help to us. Have you forgotten she rescued us from the crash?"

"She was of assistance, but now she is a hindrance."

"What's that supposed to mean?" Fiona frowned.

"You will need to leave." Darrogh crossed his arms over his chest. "Your presence puts the men in danger."

Anger seared through Fiona. She'd been foolish to trust these guys. All their talk of protection and honor were just words in the end. She fought back her tears. She wouldn't give them the satisfaction of knowing that she was upset.

"So you'd like me to take off?" Fiona stood and grabbed her bag, shoving stuff into it as fast as her hands would move. "I wish you luck with your life here on earth."

"There is no reason for you to rush." Darrogh's voice was firm. "We will find you a means of transportation first."

"Really?" Fiona shook her head and went into the washroom, gathering her toiletries before returning to the room. "You seem very sure of your decision."

"I am second in command."

Fiona pulled her phonebook from the side pocket of her pack. She thumbed through the pages until she found the number she wanted. "So that means that your judgment is always right?"

She picked up the phone and started to dial, but before she could finish, Darrogh had taken the receiver from her and slammed it down.

"You will not contact anyone."

"You don't control me."

Fiona had had enough of this arrogant brute. She needed to make a phone call and he wasn't going to stop her. She'd vowed she'd never let a man walk all over her again and she'd meant it. He might frighten the others, but not her. She brought her knee up and slammed him with all her strength. Darrogh's eyes widened and he bent over in pain.

Ardal walked into the room at that moment.

Fiona's heart started to beat frantically. Her eyes devoured him. She longed to run to him, but she doubted the others would approve. Ardal looked at her and then at Darrogh.

"What has happened?"

"I was trying to make a phone call and this brute stopped me. I don't care how much danger you're in, I won't be thrown onto the streets without calling for help."

Ardal stopped her with his hand. "Sit." Then he looked at Firbin. "Explain."

"Darrogh told Fiona that she was a hindrance and must leave." Firbin's voice was hesitant. "She tried to make a call and he stopped her. That is when she kneed him."

Ardal smiled at Fiona and then looked back at the other men. All of them had averted their eyes from Darrogh and were waiting for his decision. He looked at his second in command and sighed.

"I did not order Fiona away."

"It is not proper." Darrogh's voice was hoarse, and he winced as he stood upright. "We will of course get her transportation."

"I vowed to protect her; as did Firbin." Ardal's voice was quiet. Fiona shivered as the silence in the room grew.

"My order was not based on emotion." Darrogh's voice held contempt.

"You would dishonor a woman and ignore a Hunter's vow?"

"I protect the men. This planet's effect on us is not to be trusted."

Ardal moved so fast that at first Fiona didn't believe it had happened. One second Darrogh was standing and the next he was slumped against the wall. Blood flowed from his lip and his legs were sprawled out in front of him. The other men looked away except Catal who seemed fascinated by the argument.

"It is not your place to judge the decisions of your leader. You are unworthy of command." Ardal's words were clipped. "No matter where a Hunter lives, honor must never be forgotten. If you cannot respect this, then you are relieved of your command."

Fiona expected Darrogh to argue, but the man seemed content, even relieved with Ardal's actions. He nodded and smiled.

She wrapped her arms around her middle to stop her shaking. Did a Hunter always question his commander's orders or was it only because they were in a strange land. It was as if they needed to respect the brute strength of their leader in order to follow.

Ardal walked over to Darrogh and held out his hand. Darrogh took the offered hand and levered himself up. For a second there was a silent communication between the men and then Ardal was leading Darrogh over to her.

"You have already met Fiona." Ardal helped her to her feet. "We are bonded. She has not interfered with my judgement or my leadership. I am still Ardal, the last of the clan Rioge, leader of the remaining Hunters. You will obey my command."

"Yes." Darrogh glanced at Fiona. "I am uncertain of this planet."

"Do you trust me?"

"You are a leader of great strength and honor. I fear this place has affected you."

"Perhaps, but that does not alter my command."

"Understood." Darrogh rubbed his chin. "I allowed fear to cloud my judgement."

"Earth has shown us that many of our legends may be real." Ardal glanced at his men. "I think we should accept that other things could be possible."

The tension in the room seemed to ease as the two men talked. A moment of upheaval had been replaced with understanding and dialogue. It was fascinating how these men worked together. Their rules and duty were woven into a fabric that allowed them to move as one.

"Now give the correct order."

Darrogh turned to Fiona and gave her a slight bow of his head. "We need to move away from here. Ardal fears it will not be safe for you to come with us. Is there someplace or someone you can go to that is trustworthy?"

Fiona looked at Ardal, but his face gave nothing away. Disappointment threatened to drown her, but she forced it back. If Ardal wanted her to leave, then she would. The last thing she wanted was to endanger him or his men. She had delayed their escape too long. It was time that she stood on her own two feet.

It was better this way.

It was a clean break before anything had begun.

Who was she kidding? It felt as if part of her was being ripped away. A future between them was impossible. They were on the run and he was from another planet.

"I'll call my sister. She lives in the city."

"Are you safe there?" Ardal's voice was clipped.

"I don't think David knows where she lives." Fiona shrugged. "Besides, I've been in hiding for almost a year. Maybe he's decided to stalk someone else."

"What about the Women's Underground Network?"

"I'll contact them from my sister's house." Fiona took a deep breath. "I'll be fine. You and your men have done more than enough for me. You have to get yourselves spread out and away from any possible threats."

Ardal nodded. "I will take you to your sister." Then he turned to the other men. "We are dividing ourselves into groups of four and five. Each group has an assigned city. You are to make your way there and wait for commands."

The other men nodded their understanding before Ardal continued. "Darrogh will take Oisen, Padrig, and Rork. They are to go east. Catal, Firbin, and Niail will come with me. We are heading south."

"You'll need identification for that." Catal spoke for the first time.

"That is why I want you with me." Ardal walked to the other man and put his hand on his shoulder. "We rely on your expertise of this planet to get us through the security systems."

Catal nodded. "It will be my honor."

There was a spark of respect in Ardal's eyes. "You three will stay here until I return. If there are supplies we need for the trip, Catal can get them. Any questions?"

"No."

Ardal nodded to the men. "Until we are together again, Hunters true and right."

"By Cygnus and Warrior, we will succeed." The men answered in unison.

Ardal motioned for Fiona to follow him. She picked up her backpack and left the room with him. She refused to look at him. Her emotions were too close to the surface to trust. Instead, she kept her eyes straight ahead. The sooner she put distance between herself and Ardal, the better.

"You have no need to hurry." Ardal's voice was close beside her. "My men will wait for me."

"The sooner I'm at Karen's, the better." Fiona forced her voice to remain indifferent. "You have to get to safety."

"I will not be secure if you are in danger." Ardal took her arm and led her to a black sedan.

"Nonsense." Fiona stopped and waited for Ardal to open the door. Once inside she took a deep breath. It was crazy to think he owed her anything. No matter what he said, they had just met. It was time to move on with her life. She'd never forget him, though.

He climbed in behind the driver's wheel and paused before putting the key in the ignition. He turned to her. She tried to smile, but failed. He grabbed her chin and leaned forward, brushing his lips across hers. Fire sparked through her. Just a brief touch and her body came to life. His lips lingered, moving back and forth, his tongue gliding across the seam of her mouth until she groaned and opened for him.

She was lost. She drank from him as he did from her. They surrendered to the joy of being one with each other without thought of the past or the future. The present was all that mattered. The kiss ended with a sigh. Ardal put his forehead against hers.

"Do not doubt me." Ardal's voice was husky with emotion. "You are essential to me. I am part of you and it will always be so."

Fiona nodded. "I understand that you have huge responsibilities and your men must come first. I shudder when I think what the military had in store for us. I wouldn't want that for anyone."

"You are unique for the people of this planet." Ardal moved away and started the engine. "These days apart have been a lesson about the problems of this place."

"There are others like me." Fiona sighed. The world was full of selfish, cruel people, but there were many more that were giving and kind. "You will find that out over time."

"Perhaps." Ardal pulled out of the parking lot. "There was a reason we were bonded though, and I am grateful."

The drive to Karen's house was less than half an hour. When they reached her small house in the north end of the city Fiona's stomach clenched. Ardal's face was blank. The Hunter was back.

She knocked at the door and Karen opened it almost immediately. Her eyes widened when she recognized Fiona and then she threw her arms around her, hugging, laughing, and crying at the same time.

"Where have you been?" Karen held Fiona at arm's length and looked at her with tears in her eyes. "It's been over a year."

"I couldn't help it." Fiona started to edge out of her sister's arms. She turned to Ardal. "This is my sister Karen. Karen, this is Ardal."

"Nice." Karen grinned at him. "At least my little sister wasn't lonely."

Ardal frowned. "I do not understand."

"Seriously?" Karen looked at Fiona with a raised eyebrow.

"We only met a couple of days ago." Fiona cleared her throat. "Is it possible for me to stay with you?"

"Of course." Karen opened the door wide and invited them in. Ardal turned back to his car, but Karen grabbed his arm. "Not so soon, big guy. We need to get acquainted. Let me get some coffee."

Karen went to the kitchen and left them in the entryway. Fiona almost laughed at the expression of confusion on Ardal's face. She led him into the living room.

"It's customary to talk a bit when meeting someone's family. Trust me, no one likes it, but you'll survive. My sister is easier to deal with than my parents."

"Why do I need to deal with them?" Ardal put emphasis on the word deal.

"It's just a saying." Fiona pushed her sister's cat aside and sat on the tattered brown couch. She patted the place beside her and Ardal sat, but didn't take his eyes from the cat.

"Why is that creature inside?"

"It's a pet." Fiona bent and captured the cat in her arms before depositing it on Ardal's lap. "Don't you have animals that you keep around you?"

"Animals are for food."

"Don't let my sister hear you say that." Fiona leaned closer to Ardal. "Personally I like dogs, but she can't abide their barking."

"Dogs?"

"They look a little like the wolves I showed you."

"Surely you would not keep such a vicious animal close?" Ardal pushed the cat off his lap. It hissed and then jumped to the floor. Obviously the two would not become friends.

"They were domesticated eons ago. They actually have a use, either as guard dogs, or helping farmers with their livestock."

Ardal gave her a steady look that spoke volumes. She could tell there was something else he wanted to do more than discuss cats and dogs. A tingle began to spread through her fingers. She itched to touch his face; to feel the warmth of his skin beneath her fingertips; to caress his strong jaw. A shudder of yearning raced through her.

The shrill of the telephone broke the spell.

Fiona could hear Karen answer, but her eyes were still focused on Ardal. All she wanted was to experience the wonder of his lips on hers, once more before he left. Who knew if they would ever see each other again? He might find another woman, or his men might convince him to forget about her. It wasn't as if he didn't have bigger problems to deal with besides her.

"Never," he whispered. His voice was so low that at first she thought she had imagined it.

He clasped her hand in his and raised it to his mouth, letting his lips lightly caress and his tongue tease a moan of longing from her. She bit her lip. This was crazy to sit in her sister's house and burn to make love with a man she had just met.

"That was work." Karen spoke from the doorway. She was pulling on a light jacket and grabbed her purse from the nearby table. "I have to fill in for someone who's sick. I'm afraid we'll have to delay this get-to-know-you chat for another time."

"How long will you be?" Fiona tried to keep the anxiety from her voice.

"An hour, no more." Karen pushed her hair out over her jacket collar. "They've found someone to fill in, but they'll be delayed a bit. I live the closest, so they call me in emergencies."

"I should leave." Ardal pushed himself up from the couch.

"Stay." Karen waved him back down. "Make yourself at home."

Chapter 19

The door slammed shut on Karen's last words. It was so like her sister, always on the run, never finding the time to listen. Fiona heaved a sigh and turned to Ardal. She leaned in to kiss him and he didn't disappoint.

He pulled her close, letting his mouth and hands show his desperate need of her. Fiona let his hunger wash over her, answering with an equally frantic desire to keep him near. This might be the last time she would hold him.

"I must stop or I will never leave you." Ardal's voice was a husky whisper.

"I don't want you to go." Fiona had never begged in her life, but if she didn't move away soon she'd start. She knew he'd stay if she asked, but she couldn't. His men needed him.

"Ask." Ardal captured her lips again. "I cannot refuse you."

"Don't tempt me." Fiona released a shaky breath. "I'll be safe with Karen."

"I cannot leave you like this." Ardal groaned. "I have a duty to protect you."

Fiona shook her head. "Your men need you."

"You should come with us."

"I'll hold you up." Fiona pushed back the pain of leaving Ardal. "Besides, they don't want me."

"I am still their leader."

"And you shouldn't have to prove it because of me." Fiona pushed away from the couch. "Knowing you and your men are safe is the only way I'll have peace."

"This is only for a short time." Ardal stood and went to the door. "Once we are across the border I will have Catal make documents for you. Then I will come back for you."

"I'll be waiting." Fiona swallowed the lump in her throat. "If I have to move I'll let Karen know where I've gone."

"I will find you by your thoughts." Ardal looked at her with unblinking eyes for several minutes before turning and leaving.

Fiona let out the breath she had been holding. She knew he'd been memorizing her, just as she had him. Soon they would be able to be together, but now it was more important for him to be safe.

She went back to the living room and straightened the couch before wandering to the kitchen. She was restless and looking for an answer. The loss of Ardal gnawed at her until she felt hollow. She filled the kettle and put it on the stove. Maybe something hot would take away the bone deep ice inside her.

The chill of Ardal's leaving.

The chill of fear.

No part of her believed that David had really stopped looking. Tomorrow she would have to contact the Women's Underground Network and find another life. The only consolation was that Ardal would be able to find her if he wanted to. He would be able to hear her thoughts and connect to her. She would never be truly alone again.

Her sister came home an hour later. By then Fiona had composed herself enough to put on a bright welcome. Karen took one look at her and shook her head before dumping a bag full of groceries on the counter. She unloaded the bag before turning to Fiona.

"You're not fooling me. Where's the hunk?"

"Ardal had to get back to his job." Fiona decided that was the best explanation. "Besides we only met a couple of days ago."

"I'll bet." Karen leaned back against the counter. "Where the hell have you been for the last year? Mom and Dad are beside themselves with worry. I already phoned them and let them know the prodigal had returned."

Fiona groaned. "I didn't want them to know. That's why I came to you. I thought I could trust you."

"You can." Karen put the milk and eggs into the fridge. "I've got your best interest in mind. I'm glad you came home. I hope this means you've seen the truth about David. The man only wanted what was best for you, but like always you were too dramatic. Quitting med school and running away. Honestly Fiona, you acted crazy."

"I didn't imagine David's behavior." Fiona hugged her arms to herself. "I don't understand why none of you believe me."

Karen leaned against the counter "Look I can recognize a jerk when I see one. David was intense, but he wasn't abusive."

"How do you know?" Fiona's fingers dug into her skin. "He made damn sure no one saw him in action. I was the only one who bore the evidence of his brutality."

Karen rolled her eyes. "You wouldn't understand brutality if it bit you in the ass. The man was in love with you."

"David doesn't know the meaning of love."

"Look if you didn't like the man that's fine by me, but don't go off about abuse." Karen tapped her index finger on the counter. "And you sure as hell didn't have to cut your family out of your life."

"I had no choice."

Fiona sighed and turned away from Karen. There was no point in continuing this discussion. It always ended with her being in the wrong. All her family saw was that David was a successful doctor.

The doorbell rang and the knot in her stomach tightened. Surely he hadn't found her yet. She swung back to Karen and looked around for a weapon. She reached for one of the knives out of the knife block, but Karen stopped her.

"It's only Mom and Dad." Karen shook her head. "You really are a mess. I'd have thought your year away would have helped you see sense."

Her parent's arrival was bitter sweet. On one hand she was glad to see them, but after their initial joy, their criticism started to weigh heavily. She loved them dearly, but their struggle to better their life and ensure their children had a bright future showed in their parenting. Fiona had once believed in their vision, but David had cured her of that. Now all she wanted was to be loved.

"Where have you been?" Her mother's breathy voice demanded once she was sitting in the living room.

"Safe."

"You couldn't call?" Her father frowned. "Your mother's been worried sick. We didn't even know whether you were alive."

"I left you a note."

Fiona twisted her hands in her lap. This was more difficult than anything she'd imagined. She'd foolishly expected them to be glad that she was safe. She hadn't expected their anger.

"A lot of good a note does." Her father glared at her. "I was almost tempted not to come and see you after your sister called, but your mother wanted to forgive you."

"Forgive me?" Fiona tried to keep the astonishment from her voice. "I didn't do anything wrong."

"You've disappointed us." Her mother held a tissue to her nose and sniffed. "We were bragging to all our friends about our daughter the doctor and then you disappear before you could take the final exams."

"So you're angry because I didn't finish med school?" Fiona shook her head. "I was trying to escape from David."

Her father stopped the conversation with a chop of his hand. "You're a silly girl, but still our daughter. Now that you've returned you can sit for your exams."

Just like that they'd summed up her life. It didn't matter that David would be waiting for her at the med school or that this time he might actually kill her. Their only concern was that she not disappoint them. Why had she expected a year's absence to change them?

Karen prepared supper and by the time her parents left Fiona was exhausted. She was past caring what her parents wanted. She didn't have the energy to fight them any longer. She needed sleep. After the dishes were cleared she made her way to the guest bedroom and collapsed on top of the covers.

She slept soundly until her door crashed open and she was dragged from bed. Fear and panic clamoured inside her. She landed on the floor with a thud. She was still half asleep, but she knew there was only one person who would treat her so violently.

David.

"I've found you now."

A shiver of dread scraped across her spine.

There was no mistaking the voice. It still haunted her nightmares. Strong hands yanked at her shoulders and gripped her with a fierce, painful hold. She was hauled to her feet and pulled from the room. She found Karen cowering on the landing. Her face was red and puffy on one side. She reached for her, but David yanked her away.

"I've had enough sisterly love for one evening." David's hand whipped hard against Karen's cheek sending her head back against the floor with a vicious bang. "No one has the right to keep you from me. You're mine."

Fiona's eyes widened as she stared at Karen, willing her to move. Her sister lay still against the floor, her hair spilled out about her. Nausea overwhelmed her and she fought to keep down the bile that rose in her throat. Dear God, please don't let her be dead.

Fiona struggled to reach Karen, but David's iron grip wouldn't release her. "Let me go."

David hauled her close to him, his hot breath feathering across her face. "You belong to me."

"Never." Fiona shook her head. "That's something you've made up in your mind."

"You refuse to see that we were meant to be together." David shook her. "You forced me to do all the work. Do you know how exhausting that is?"

"I never asked you to like me."

"You're young. You don't understand what love is."

"This isn't love." Fiona struggled to free herself, but he held her firm.

"Running got you nowhere." David threw her over his shoulder and stomped down the stairs. "I knew you couldn't stay away forever. You're lucky that I'm a patient man."

She looked back up at Karen. She hadn't moved. Fiona shuddered as she took one last look. This would be the last time that she would see her sister. David wasn't going to let her live. His anger and insanity were out of control. He had gone over the edge.

Once outside, he threw her into the back of his car. She struggled to move away, but he grabbed her hand and snapped the end of a steel handcuff onto her wrist. He attached the other end of the manacle to the base of the front seat. She was forced to lay on the backseat to prevent the cuff from ripping into the skin of her wrist. David slammed the door shut and then climbed into the driver's seat. Seconds later they were speeding off. It was hopeless to fight. Her fate had been decided.

She would die this night.

Her heart cried for what might have been, for all the dreams that would never come true. Most of all she mourned the loss of love. She would never feel a man's loving embrace again. Her last moments would be filled with violence and anger. She fought back a sob of regret. She wouldn't let that happen. Even if she never escaped, she could control what she would see in those last minutes of life. She would focus on love.

She would focus on Ardal.

She'd let his love and strength surround her.

The car came to an abrupt stop sending her flying off into the rear of the front seats. She groaned as her back hit the bump on the car floor. If she were lucky she'd live long enough to see the bruises.

David peered over the headrest. "We're almost there."

A blast of warm air let her know that the door had been opened. David twisted her back onto the seat before pulling her sleeve up on her arm. He held a needle in his other hand. A sharp burning sensation seared her bicep.

"That should keep you quiet until I'm ready."

"What are you going to do?" Fiona couldn't keep the fear from her voice.

"I tried to love you, but you refused." David pulled her sleeve down. "Now you'll die like all the rest."

"I don't understand." Fiona swallowed back her horror.

"It's quite simple." David pushed the needle protector up. "I thought you might be different, but you're not. I'll kill you like the others, slowly and painfully until you beg for my love."

He slammed the door and within seconds, the car was moving again. She felt the dragging action of the drug he'd given her start to take effect. Her eyelids were heavy and she fought to keep them open. She wanted to remember Ardal's face as long as possible.

His beloved face was clear in her mind's eye.

Now when it was too late, she realized how much she loved him. He was truly the only man she would ever love. It was fitting that he would be the last man in her thoughts. She wouldn't let David win. She would block his evil and focus on Ardal. Her last thoughts would be of him. At least he would know how she really felt as she sent her message to him.

"I love you," she repeated until the words blurred and her mind clouded.

Ardal was the last word on her lips as the world darkened and her thoughts ceased.

Chapter 20

Darkness encompassed the vehicle and his heart. For the first time in his life, Ardal felt detached from his men. He was a Hunter of the clan Rioge, the last leader of his breed and yet he could only think of Fiona. The pain of leaving her gnawed at his gut. He knew his men came first, but he should never have let them convince him to do something that felt so wrong.

Despite what Darrogh had implied, he knew she was not a distraction. She was his anchor. She grounded him. He might not have needed that in the past, but since bonding he realized that it was necessary to have a constant connection with her. He cursed himself for not realizing this earlier, but it was all so new.

No Hunter had pair bonded before.

There was no rule or code to follow.

He was floundering in a strange land with no guidance. He suddenly understood much clearer what the stranded Hunters had endured. It was worse for them because they hadn't finished their training. They had been children.

Ardal sighed and looked out the window. No matter how he felt, he had to put it behind him and get his men to safety. They had dispersed and were trying to find new lives. Catal had made arrangements for his group to have papers and identities. With these in place, they could travel to the far reaches of this planet.

A wave of nausea hit Ardal with a piercing ache that twisted his gut. He grimaced and clutched his side. Never had he felt anguish like this, not in the worse battle, not when tortured, nor when punished as a boy. Never.

He gripped the door handle until his knuckles were white. The nausea lessened, but the agony grew. He took several deep breaths and forced the sensation away. Years of training had made him adept at ignoring discomfort. Every Hunter had the ability.

The torment grew more intense. There was only one explanation. This was not his pain.

Fiona was in agonizing distress.

His bonding meant that he felt what she did, but the intensity of it could only mean one thing. She was in peril. Worse, she was probably close to dying.

"We must return."

Catal glanced round from the front. "We're leaving the city. We need to put distance between us."

"Fiona is in danger. I have to find her."

Firbin moved the vehicle into the right lane and took the next exit.

"You can't just turn around. The military are looking for us."

"Ardal is leader. I obey my leader."

Catal exhaled a heavy sigh. "This is nuts. What don't you understand about the danger we're in?"

"We are always in danger." Niail spoke from beside Ardal. "A Hunter obeys."

Catal turned and looked at him for a few seconds. "You're serious."

Niail gave him a steady gaze. "Ardal has always led us true."

Catal shook his head. "I hope that you still feel the same when we're captured."

"I do not put my men in unnecessary danger. I will return on my own. You may continue the journey without me." Ardal kept his voice low.

"No." Niail shook his head. "We follow where you lead."

"This is to protect my pair bond."

Firbin stopped at a red light and signaled a right turn. "I made a vow to Fiona also. A Hunter does not betray his word."

"You would never let us face danger on our own." Niail added.

Catal rubbed his face with his hands. "It's three against one. Short of jumping out of this car, I have no choice but to go along with you."

"You are young, but you learn quickly." Niail's voice was dry.

"I'm older than you." Catal's voice reverberated in the closed vehicle.

"Only in years." Niail's voice held a hint of humour. "Your life as a Hunter begins today."

It took them fifteen minutes to reach Fiona's sister's house. They pulled into the driveway and Ardal jumped out of the vehicle. The others followed and together they went to the front door. It was open by several inches. Ardal steadied his breathing and calmed his adrenaline surge as he prepared for battle.

They entered the house with soft steps, Ardal motioning his men to spread out and search. The ground floor was cleared before they started up the stairs. That was when he saw Karen on the upper landing. She was sprawled out as if dead and he feared the worse. He knelt beside her as his men began their search of the upper floor.

He shook Karen's shoulder and was greeted by a groan. She was alive. When the others returned, she was struggling to sit up on her elbows. His men moved away from her, forming a circle as they stood looking down, hands behind their backs, and legs spread.

Ardal was the first to speak. "Is Fiona here?"

Niail shook his head. "The house is empty except for a small furry animal I found in a closet. There was a struggle in one of the bedrooms."

Ardal sucked in his anger and frustration. Fiona needed him to be clear minded if she were going to survive. He turned to Karen. "What happened?"

She grimaced and sat up. "The bastard took her. I should have believed her when she told me that he was abusive, but he's a doctor, for God's sake."

"How long?"

"Maybe ten minutes ago." Karen held her head in her hands. "I tried to stop him, but he knocked me out. Wait until I get my hands on him. He'll regret the day he messed with a Nevins."

"You would hurt him?" Niail's surprised voice broke the silence that had followed Karen's words.

"Damn right." Karen stood with a grunt. "Give me a knife and I'll see he never reproduces again."

Ardal smiled. Fiona's sister had spirit. "We need to find him first."

"I probably have an address for him somewhere. If not, the internet will help."

"Where is your computer?" Catal stepped forward. "I'm an expert in finding people."

"Is that so?" Karen shrugged and started down the stairs. "I have one in the kitchen."

While Karen searched through a drawer in her desk, Catal attacked the laptop. After getting the spelling of David's name correct, he started hitting the keys furiously. Within seconds he had his home address, the hospital that he worked at, and his office. Karen had no success with her address book. Instead she moved beside Catal and watched as his fingers spewed out information.

"That's amazing." She leaned closer to the screen. "Isn't that a secure site?"

Catal grunted. "Nothing is protected."

"I can see that." Karen's voice was dry as she moved away. She looked at Ardal. "What are you going to do?"

"Find Fiona."

"I'm coming with you."

"Not possible." Ardal knew the operation might involve force and he didn't want to be responsible for another female. Keeping Fiona safe would be a hard enough task.

"She's my sister." Karen's voice rose. "It's my fault I opened the door to him."

Ardal shook his head. "She is my pair bond. I am responsible, not you. I will keep her safe."

Karen frowned. "Your what?"

He should have kept his mouth shut. Now Karen was bound to ask questions he could not answer. "We are connected. Fiona knows that I will come for her."

Karen raised an eyebrow and crossed her arms over her chest. "How?"

Catal interrupted before he was forced to explain. "He has a small rental unit in a warehouse complex. It's in the industrial district."

"Is that normal?" Ardal turned to look at the computer.

Catal shook his head. "He has a separate storage near his office. The only reason to have such a unit would be if he were starting a new enterprise. I see no evidence of that from his online activities."

The world might be different, but the behaviour was the same. The patterns of a coward did not change. He had been a Hunter for too many years, and on too many diverse planets not to recognize the signs of a private lair. Deviants always needed a secret place to hide their activities.

"How far."

"Less than half an hour."

"Weapons?"

"We have a stash near here."

Ardal nodded. "Good."

He motioned to Firbin, who left to start the van. Catal had brought up a map on the computer. Ardal glanced at it to get his bearings before Catal closed the laptop, unplugged it, and hitched it under his arm.

"I'm going with you guys. No one takes my computer without me." Karen grabbed a set of keys from her countertop and then followed Catal out the kitchen door.

"Stay." Ardal blocked Karen's exit from the house. "You are hurt."

"She's family."

"We do not take women on our missions." Niail's voice was firm.

"Never?" Karen's voice was doubtful.

Ardal shook his head. "My men do not need to worry about your safety. You will endanger the job."

"I've a right to be there."

"We will let you know when Fiona is safe." Ardal took the computer from Catal and handed it back to Karen.

"What if you're too late?" Karen's words ended with a sob.

"She is still alive." Ardal motioned Niail and Catal to leave. "My men are trained and experienced with situations like this. You must trust."

Karen nodded. "Should I call the police?"

"Wait until we contact you." Ardal turned to leave. He knew Karen doubted him, but he had to get to Fiona. He didn't have the time to reassure her.

The men climbed into the van. When the doors were shut, Firbin punched in the address on the direction system and started driving. He had them at the weapons depot in a matter of minutes.

Firbin's eyes widened when he saw the stash of weapons. "You are well prepared."

"It's how we've survived." Catal started handing assault rifles to Niail, who stashed them in the back of the van.

"I am thankful that you have these." Ardal grabbed a small handgun and pushed it into the back of his pants. "It will make the operation easier."

He could kill David with his bare hands, but he wasn't taking any chances with Fiona's life. He would go in with as much force as possible and worry about the clean up later.

The neighborhood of David's rental unit had few streetlights. Even fewer had lights still working. In daylight it would have looked rundown and grimy. The inky black of night did nothing to improve it. They parked a block away.

Ardal got out of the van and stood still for a few seconds. He sniffed the air. It was humid and rank with the odor of uncollected garbage. He blocked the night sounds as he narrowed his focus on the building that housed David's rental space.

The area was deserted.

Ardal noted the position of the security cameras on the building. They were easy enough to deal with. David's unit was number 27. It was located right in the middle. Their first obstacle would be the locked gates and the security guard. A lack of traffic in the area meant that driving up to the gate was not an option.

It was a standard stealth operation. Ardal assessed his route and prepared for battle. Catal threw out black face coverings and they chose weapons.

Ardal pulled his face mask down.

His men waited for his commands.

Few directions were needed for such a basic manoeuvre. Catal was new though, and Ardal motioned for him to stay near. Niail took a position out of camera range and then shot out the offending units one by one. It took a couple of seconds before the security guard reacted. He moved out of his booth by the gate. By that time Firbin had scaled the fence.

The man was unconscious with one blow.

Firbin dragged him back into his cubicle and then opened the gates. They ran through quickly, securing their position before moving on to the sentry house. The guard was now lying on his side, his hands bound in front of him and his mouth gagged. Once he was conscious, he would be able to free himself easily.

Time was limited.

They moved to number 27.

The men stood on either side of the door and Ardal shot the handle off. He kicked the door in and rushed the building. His men followed close behind, taking spots against the wall. They were in a small reception room.

Boxes were stacked against the exterior and down the center of the room. They formed a hallway of sorts, with two doors at the end. There was a desk against the far end and what looked like a computer on it.

The room was empty.

Fiona was not there.

Chapter 21

Had they come to the wrong place?

Ardal reached out for Fiona with his mind. She was near. He could feel her heartbeat, but no words reached him. He pushed back his fear and moved into the room. He paused after each step using all the stealth his training provided. His men followed close behind.

Silence was the only thing that greeted them.

Ardal motioned for Niail to move to the first door. He gripped the handle and when Ardal nodded he pulled it open. It led to a small storage closet. Niail swept his weapon around the inside and then shook his head before closing the door.

He moved to the next door. Ardal took a deep breath and calmed his heart rate. His men signalled their readiness and then he nodded. The door was flung open and they entered before they could take another breath.

The site that met Ardal sent a shiver of dread up his spine. Never in his twenty years of fighting had he ever been so sickened. Fiona was here, but she was not moving. She lay tied to a table in the center of the room.

Cases and tabletops were filled with metal instruments and tools of different shapes. Chains, ropes, and pulleys hung from the ceiling, dangling in the breeze caused by an electric fan. There was only one light glaring bright above Fiona. All else was shrouded in shadows.

The odor of death permeated everything.

A man about Ardal's height stood amidst this macabre scene. He was wearing a plastic coat that was spattered with blood. Ardal swallowed the bile that rose in his throat. After he had killed the bastard he would have time enough to be sick. Fiona's heart still beat. There was hope.

"Who the hell are you?"

"I think the question should be what are we?" Ardal's voice was a low growl.

"Semantics." The doctor wasted no time in moving to Fiona. He pulled a syringe from the workspace beside her and aimed it at her arm. "Leave now and there will be no questions asked. Stay and you can watch her die."

"That is not happening." Ardal nodded to Niail. One shot and the needle shattered. "Let her go."

David's eyes narrowed. He pulled Fiona down beside him. Using the table as a shield he cut her ties and then dragged her in front of him until he found the protection of a wheeled red metal chest. He pushed the container in front of him as he moved toward the open door. Ardal kept his eyes on his quarry while Catal and Niail moved into position on either side of David.

"Let her go." Ardal took a step toward the cart that David was crouched behind. "This is between us men."

"Four against one?" David snickered. "You must think I'm a fool."

"Only one Hunter is needed to defeat a coward."

David pushed the cart toward the door. He used the cover of the metal to help his escape. "I have no intention of being caught."

"We will not touch you." Ardal did not add that the man would be dead before they reached him. It was a given. No Hunter would handle an aberration like the doctor. His dead carcass would be left for scavengers to tear apart.

"So you will just let me walk out of here."

"No."

The doctor snorted. "At least you're honest. Why are you here? What does Fiona have to do with you?"

"I am sworn to protect her."

"Very heroic, but your services aren't necessary. Fiona is mine." The tool chest's wheels squeaked a few inches closer to the door.

"Hunters keep their vows." Ardal nodded and a single shot rang out. Niail's aim was true. David fell backwards, with Fiona still clutched near his chest.

Ardal threw the toolbox against the wall as he rushed to Fiona. She was still breathing, but barely. He pulled her away from David and gathered her into his arms. Her body was limp, her heartbeat slow, but she was alive. He stood and surveyed the room. The grizzly scene would speak for itself.

They would leave it and let the authorities deal with the fallout. They backed out of the room. Ardal followed close behind with Fiona held tight.

Firbin was the first to speak. "Is she alive?"

"Yes." Ardal moved outside.

They needed to get away before the authorities arrived. The guard would be conscious soon. They reached the van within seconds and when Niail reached for Fiona, Ardal shook his head. He would not relinquish his hold. She was his pair bond and would remain in his arms. They scrambled into the vehicle.

Firbin spun the van around and sped away from the warehouse. They passed their weapons back to Niail who began to disassemble and hide them in the rear. Within minutes they were on the highway. Fiona groaned and Ardal tightened his grip on her.

He tried to mind connect, but there was only confusion and darkness. He sent her thoughts of healing and love. It was all he could do until they could get the medical attention she needed.

"Where?" Firbin's voice was taut. They were still in military mode.

"The border is out." Catal pulled a map from his pocket. "We have a safe house about an hour west."

"Fiona needs a doctor." Ardal kept his voice low.

"Too risky." Catal turned to look at him. "The safe house has all the supplies we need."

Ardal looked down at Fiona. She could have been sleeping; her body relaxed in his arms, her breathing steady, but shallow, her heart beat slow, but strong. The man in him wanted to get her help. The leader knew the escape and safety of everyone was his main concern. The quicker that was accomplished, the safer Fiona would be. He nodded to Catal.

"Do it."

Catal grunted and then leaned toward Firbin to give directions.

At that moment Fiona groaned.

Ardal's breath caught in his throat as he willed her to waken. Her eyelids fluttered and then opened. His hand shook as he brushed a few strands of hair away from her face. She stared up at him and then smiled.

"I knew you'd come." She yawned and then snuggled closer. "He gave me a shot of something. I'm sleepy."

"You are safe." Ardal's voice was a hoarse whisper.

"Don't let me go." Fiona's eyes fluttered shut, but her last words were audible for all to hear. "I love you."

Ardal sucked in his breath and pulled her close. His heart constricted as he thought of what might have happened if he had been too late. The grizzly scene of David's warehouse flashed through his mind. He was a warrior used to dealing with death and blood, but he could not have borne the anguish if something had happened to Fiona.

Never again would he leave her in danger.

"We need to contact Fiona's sister to let her know she's safe." Ardal looked up at Catal. "Can we do it without being found?"

Catal nodded. "I will take care of it."

It took less than an hour to arrive at the safe house. It was located a few miles from a small village. The house was made of brick and painted wood. It was old, lacking the pristine newness of the massive subdivisions that they had passed along the way. It sat on a hill and was surrounded by fields on all sides. To the north was a small woodlot. No one could approach without being seen. It was perfect.

Catal directed Firbin to park the vehicle in a small outbuilding and then led the way to the house. Inside it had an open kitchen and living area, but with the push of a button, a section of kitchen cupboards slid open to reveal a hidden room that was filled with weapons, computers, and communication equipment. Niail stowed the bag of weapons from the van on the floor.

Ardal placed Fiona on the couch. "Get the medical equipment."

Catal pulled a large black chest from the hidden room and rolled it to him. "Let me."

With skilled hands, he took Fiona's vitals and then began to inspect her from head to toe. Ardal's fists tightened as he watched Catal begin his examination. He forced back his resentment of another man touching her and moved aside. It was obvious Catal was a trained medic. Fiona was in good hands. Now he needed to focus on the safety of his men.

"Have we heard from the others?" He moved to the entrance of the hidden room. Niail was pulling other weapons from the wall and putting them in another carry bag.

"The radio cannot be trusted." Niail looked up from the bag. "It is best they hear from you."

Ardal nodded and took a deep breath. He relaxed his body and sent his thoughts to his men. Within seconds he had replies. Everyone had been successful in their mission, except him. Then he connected with Lorcan and advised him of their situation.

"Everyone is safe." Ardal walked into the living room. "How is Fiona?"

"She's stable." Catal was packing away his equipment. "She needs to sleep off whatever drug she was given. There's a bedroom upstairs. It would be best for her to rest there."

Ardal shook his head. "She stays near me."

Catal grunted. "Understood."

"Lorcan has shut down the other site. He should be here within the hour." Ardal rubbed the back of his neck. "We will make new plans then."

Firbin was standing guard at the door. "Are the others safe?"

"Yes. They have not encountered any resistance."

Niail came out of the equipment room. "How can a monster like that be allowed to live on this planet?"

"Fiona complained to the police and they refused to help." Firbin put his hands on his hips. "This would not be allowed on Cygnus."

Catal cleared his throat. "Here, a judge or jury determine if a person is guilty. The police need proof. Sometimes there isn't enough evidence, or there are points of law that aren't followed correctly, and a guilty person goes free."

"There is no honor or reason then?" Ardal's voice did not hide his shock.

Catal shook his head. "There's only the law. Many businesses and people are able to exist outside the law."

What kind of planet had they crashed onto?

They were hunted and treated no better than animals. Women were given no reverence and their orders were not obeyed. Violence seemed to be at the core of the individual's existence, not just warriors' lives. Honor was disregarded, and now this.

To knowingly let an injustice be committed and not right it was too much for a Hunter. His duty was to uphold the Sacred Code and that meant taking action against those who broke them.

"There is good." Fiona's words broke into the silence. "Many humans choose love over hate."

Ardal's heart filled with joy at the sound of her voice. He moved to her side. She was struggling to sit up and he put his arm around her back. When she was straight, she leaned her head against the couch.

"You are awake." He pushed back a strand of hair and let his fingers linger on her cheek, savoring the tingle of awareness and the flare of heat that was reflected in her eyes.

"I'm alive, thanks to you." Fiona's gaze encompassed all the men. "I am grateful that you came for me."

Ardal put his arms around Fiona and pulled her close. "No woman should have to see such a travesty, much less experience it."

Niail grunted. "Your planet allows some strange practices."

"It's not allowed, but unfortunately the police can only do so much. Serial killers like David can escape capture for many years. Even I didn't fully realize what a monster he was."

"And the killing lasts as long as they are free." Catal's lips thinned with disapproval.

"This is not like Cygnus where such a man would have been weeded out when he was young and killed." Firbin's voice was hard.

"Killed before he had done anything?" Fiona shivered. "What if he never acted out his fantasies?"

"Society must be protected at all costs." Ardal leaned his chin on Fiona's head. "It is not perfect, but at least no one has to suffer as did David's victims."

"There has to be a better way." Fiona twisted around in Ardal's arms and looked up at him. "Even though I hate to think of one life being put at risk, it's better than killing someone who might never do wrong."

"Your planet does not have the capability of seeing the evil in a person's genes. Cygnus has done this for millennium."

"True." Fiona heaved a sigh. "The best we can do is to stop it once it's begun."

Firbin frowned. "Like we did with David?"

"Even that doesn't ensure people are safe." Catal turned away with a shake of his head. "This planet has shown us only evil."

"Fiona showed us kindness." Niail spoke in a clear voice. "She took care of our sick, hid us, and helped us to escape. All this she did at great peril to herself."

"True." Firbin nodded. "She risked much to help us."

Catal cleared his throat. "There are few humans like Fiona."

"But you have known some?" Ardal raised an eyebrow. "Lorcan thinks there are no redemptive qualities on this planet."

"Lorcan has lost much." Catal eyes skittered away from Ardal's intense stare. "I now see that he has allowed that to cloud his perception and his command."

Before Ardal could continue his questioning, the distinct sound of a vehicle approaching sent the men running for weapons. Catal switched the lights off and took guard at one of the windows. Niail and Firbin stood on either side of the entryway, assault rifles readied to shoot.

Ardal planted himself in front of Fiona and braced for battle.

Chapter 22

They heard the slam of two doors and footsteps.

Fiona tried to get up, but her legs refused to move. Whatever drug David had given her was still in her system. She leaned back against the couch and swallowed her fear. Ardal would protect her.

The door swung open.

No one entered.

Seconds passed and then Catal moved from the window. "It is Lorcan."

Three newcomers entered the building. Lorcan was followed by Gur and Turlo. Fiona released the breath she'd been holding. Her insides were shaky and she was exhausted. She was too tired to deal with the constant stress of the past few days. She lay her head on the couch arm and shut her eyes.

The noise of the men greeting each other washed over her, but she was past caring. She felt Ardal's lips brush her head and then she let the world fade away. Sleep was a relief.

When she awoke, it was still dark.

Strong arms held her. Peace and love filled her. She stretched her legs and realized that she wasn't on the couch, but in a large bed. Ardal must have carried her up after the others arrived. A nightlight illuminated the small room. It was cosy and warm and most importantly, they were alone.

She twisted her head and looked up at him. Her breath caught in her throat. He was gazing at her with an intensity that she'd never seen before. His eyes, usually devoid of emotion, were brimming with love. Gone was the cold, decisive leader. In his place was a man.

A man who offered love and devotion.

Her experience with love was limited. David had dominated and tried to possess her, but he'd never loved her. Ardal was offering something she'd never had before. She was tired of running. He was her rock; her refuge. She never wanted to leave his side again. The past faded. It no longer held the power to destroy her.

Fiona saw her future in Ardal's eyes.

She liked what she saw.

"I have never asked this before." Ardal tightened his clasp on her. "Forgive me if I say the words wrong. Has your fear lessened enough for you to be with me?"

Fiona nodded. She was afraid her voice would crack if she said anything. Instead she leaned up and brushed her lips across his mouth.

"Yes." Her word a sigh as her lips touched his again.

Ardal gathered her into his arms and deepened the kiss. His tongue was insistent until she opened for him. He tantalized and caressed until she moaned with enjoyment. That was all the encouragement he need. He held the back of her head close to him and delved deeper, enticing her to follow. Time ceased as together they explored and teased until they were both panting for breath.

"Will you be my mate?" Ardal's voice was husky with passion. "You will be the only woman in my life and I vow to protect you always. My life is yours to command."

The solemnity and beauty of his words pierced her heart. Tears filled her eyes. She blinked them away and gave him a tremulous smile. "Yes."

"I will defend and honor you. I vow to bring you pleasure and happiness." Ardal stroked a finger down her cheek. "You will always be in my heart."

"I love you." A wave of joy encompassed her.

A whispered *my one true mate* touched her thoughts and then scattered. She thought she'd imagined it, until she realized Ardal was connecting to her on a higher level. His thoughts were making love just as his body moved with her. She shivered with excitement, pulsating with the thrill of his efforts.

Fiona answered him with thoughts. 'I want to make love.'

His reaction was immediate. He groaned and crushed her to him. His lips devoured her mouth and she answered with equal hunger. Passion was a living, breathing entity between them and it burned out of control. His body half covered her as he strove to meld them together.

His lips moved lower, trailing searing kisses along her jaw and neck until he reached the button of her shirt. Her body was screaming for more and yet he hesitated and looked up at her.

"Is this what you want?"

She nodded.

Words were beyond her.

His hand moved to the buttons of her shirt and undid the first and then the second. Each one was unclasped in agonizing slow motion until her shirt was open. She shrugged it off and groaned with pleasure as Ardal's fingers caressed her skin, trailing fire along the way. He explored her collar bone and rested a finger on the pulse at the base of her neck. A slight smile tilted his lips.

"You are so beautiful and alive." A shadow crossed his eyes. "I do not think I could have lived if he had killed you."

"Shush. We've been given a second chance and I'm not going to waste it."

Fiona slid her hands beneath his tee shirt, inching her fingers up taut muscles and hair roughened skin. He felt delicious. When he shivered, her body answered with a surge of triumph.

Her touch thrilled him.

Her exploration grew bold and she gripped the lower edge of his shirt and pulled it over his head. His chest was exposed in all its glory. Firm abdomen muscles and large well-developed pecs quivered as she caressed every inch of him with first her fingers and then her lips.

Scars from injuries marred the perfection of his skin, as did a tattoo on his left upper arm. It had numerous hieroglyphic-type symbols running up and down in lines. Her fingers moved across the lines, which contained at least twenty symbols. There were ten lines in total.

"What are these?"

"My missions and campaigns."

"So many?" Her eyes lifted to his, but there was no remembered pain there. Just acceptance of the life he'd been born to.

She looked at the symbols again and then moved closer so that her lips could caress them. They represented what had made him the man she loved. She would honor that. When she had finished, Ardal was stroking her jaw with his hands. He lifted her head so that he could kiss her lips again.

He built the fire gradually, letting his mouth and tongue move down to her neck in a torturous, deliberate progress. She ached for more. Ardal continued to ignite the flame within her until she twisted beneath him, her hips lifting to meet him, begging for a closer intimacy. He didn't disappoint.

He unclipped her bra, brushed his fingers across her nipples sending shards of ecstasy racing across her body. She gasped at the throbbing pulse of yearning that seared deep within her womb.

"You like that?" Ardal's voice was husky with passion.

"You know I do." Fiona moaned as Ardal flicked his tongue over her nipple.

He nibbled and soothed until she burned with need and then he suckled, sending a jolt of excitement soaring through her. She hardly noticed when he smoothed her pants and undies off her body. His mouth left her breasts and began to explore her abdomen.

His lips roamed until he reached the apex of her thighs. He hesitated a second, inhaling deeply of her scent as if savoring it, before continuing his tasting. His tongue darted out and licked her inner core until she shuddered with pleasure.

He continued to build the hunger until she could stand it no longer. Her fingers moved down to his pants and fumbled trying to undo the fastening. It wouldn't budge.

She stroked lower, feeling the rigid evidence of his arousal. Taking the palm of her hand she rubbed down its length. Ardal jerked away, his muscles trembling with tension.

"Two can play this game." Fiona purred with satisfaction. "Take your pants off. I want to see and feel you."

"Lovemaking is for the woman's enjoyment."

"It's for both of us." Fiona gazed at him, willing him to understand. "You have to trust me."

Ardal shut his eyes briefly and then nodded. "As you command." He stripped with quick, economical movements and then lay down beside her.

He was magnificent.

She ran her hand down the full length of him.

She shuddered at the piercing throb of excitement that filled her. Would she be able to accommodate him? The thought flittered through her brain for a second before Ardal's hands were working their magic again.

She surrendered to sensation.

His tongue and hands coaxed and enticed her body to a fevered pitch, leaving her panting and begging for completion. She reached for him and stroked down the long length of his arousal.

Ardal groaned. "You will unman me."

"I need you inside me." Fiona's words came in breathless gasps. "Now."

"Show me."

She pushed Ardal onto his back and straddled him. She reached between them and guided him until he was on the verge of entering her. With slow, deliberate concentration she eased herself down onto him until it felt as if he filled and stretched her whole being.

She shivered with bliss.

Then she moved.

She established an unhurried rocking motion. Her body set a rhythm that sent a luscious spiral of rapture singing through her until she could handle no more. That's when Ardal gripped her back and hips and with a smooth twist of his body swung her beneath him.

He thrust into her and then pulled out before gliding in again. He continued his leisurely strokes until Fiona was on the searing edge of climax. He captured her mouth and scream as he plunged deep, driving her over the top to exquisite ecstasy. Seconds later she felt his body shudder his fulfillment.

His weight collapsed onto her and she held him tight, letting the soft glow of the aftermath of their loving envelop and cocoon them. He grunted a protest and then shifted their bodies so they were on their sides. Languidly she let her lips roam his chest.

She couldn't remember ever feeling this euphoric.

Everything was perfect, especially this man, her mate.

"You have shown me heaven." Ardal gave her a lingering kiss.

"It was fantastic." Fiona nipped at his lips. "Where did you learn to move like that?"

"Instinct." Ardal moved his hips. "I need to pleasure you again."

Fiona laughed. "It's too soon."

"Not for me."

Another thrust and Fiona felt the hardened truth of Ardal's words deep within her. She moaned as the coil of passion gripped her again. Who was she to argue with a Hunter?

The light fingers of dawn were touching the sky when Fiona woke. It had been a night of lovemaking that had only ended a few hours ago. She would be sluggish for the rest of the day, but what was sleep compared to the paradise that she'd found in Ardal's arms. The man was inexhaustible and she had the aching muscles to prove it.

She stretched her arms over her head. She felt good. Better than she'd ever felt in her whole life. She touched Ardal's cheek. He'd made her whole. Now it was time to let him do his duty. She could face anything, knowing that he was with her.

She grabbed her pants and pulled them on.

"You need more sleep." Ardal's voice was gentle.

"It wouldn't do for your men to find us like this."

When she'd finished dressing she stood and pulled the curtains, shutting out the glow of sunrise before switching on a light. Ardal's eyes followed her every move. A shiver of awareness skittered across her body. He was hers as much as she was a part of him. There was a mutual give and take between them that would only strengthen the longer that they were together.

How could she bear it if he went away?

"I cannot leave you." Ardal stood and pulled her into his arms. "It would be like cutting out my heart."

"You're reading my thoughts again." Fiona shook her head and sighed. "I hope you're the only Hunter in my head."

Ardal frowned. "You are my pair bond and mate. No other can touch your thoughts."

"That's a relief." Fiona relaxed into his embrace. "I've got some pretty crazy stuff going on in there. You're the only man I'd share it with."

"I hold your trust sacred. I will never betray it." Ardal kissed her forehead. "Until last night I did not understand the full meaning of being mated. There is nothing that is more important."

Fiona grinned. "That's because it's new. Give it a few years and you'll be like all the other old married men."

"Married?"

"It's sort of the same as your mating, except some people get divorced."

"That does not sound good."

Fiona shook her head. "It isn't. They separate and decide not to see each other again."

"Never." Ardal's hold tightened. "Even if you do not want me, I will always honor our mating."

She swallowed the lump in her throat. "I love you, now and always."

Ardal leaned down and kissed her with a tenderness that brought tears to her eye. "We will honor your customs and marry."

Fiona blinked back her tears and nodded. "Can we? It's legally binding and would be on record. I wouldn't want it to endanger you or your men."

"Catal and the others will know how to avoid problems."

"You'd be my husband and I'd be your wife." Fiona tried to keep her excitement down. She had to think of Ardal's safety.

"This is important to you." Ardal leaned back and let his eyes roam her face.

"It would be a binding commitment that no one could sever or doubt."

Ardal nodded. "Then we will marry."

At that moment there was a pounding at the door and then Niail's voice. "We must leave."

Chapter 23

Fiona threw his clothes at him. "Get dressed," she mouthed.

He reached out and caressed her cheek. She turned her face into his palm and kissed it. A surge of emotion rushed through him.

Last night she had given him heaven.

Now he must do his duty.

Fiona gave him a quick smile and then left the room. With a grunt he pulled on his pants and shirt. The men would be waiting their orders. As much as he wished to continue pleasuring Fiona it was time to begin their lives on earth. They were Hunters and last night had shown him there was a need for them on this planet.

When he got downstairs the smell of breakfast cooking permeated the small space. Fiona was humming at the stove and Firbin was putting food on plates. He took the dish offered him and sat at the table beside Niail.

"Are the others ready?"

"We await your command."

Ardal nodded. "I need you to take Gur and Turlo with you. You are to head west and await your instructions."

"You give me the new ones?" Niail raised an eyebrow. "I am not good with trainees."

"No, but I trust you with them." Ardal bit into a piece of bread. "Once you are west, you will join with Ranon, Partlan, and Malac."

Firbin sat across from them. "What is the plan?"

"I have given thought to our purpose on this planet. It is our home now and we must find our way as Hunters."

"So we continue to do as Lorcan has?"

"No." Ardal's voice was firm. "There is no honor in the choice he made. A Hunter must always live with honor no matter where he finds himself."

"True." Niail pushed his empty plate away. "There does not seem to be much of it on this planet though."

"That is not true." Fiona leaned between Ardal and Niail and took away their plates. "You just have to look deeper to find it."

Niail watched Fiona walk to the kitchen. "I do not think I will get used to women waiting on me."

"It works both ways on earth." Ardal leaned back in his chair. "Each gives and takes. It is a fairer division."

Niail frowned. "You believe this."

"I know it." Last night had shown him how much greater the reward when it was shared. "There is still a need for Hunters though."

"What will we do?" Lorcan leaned against the kitchen island. "Honor does not put food on the table or buy weapons."

"There is much injustice and corruption here." Ardal hesitated as he tried to find the right words. "You said the law is not able to stop many of the wrongs that happen."

Lorcan nodded. "Sometimes the police and lawyers are as corrupt as the criminals they try to catch."

"That is why they need Hunters." Ardal put his hands around his coffee mug. "We can fill the void for the people who are being wronged."

Catal pulled out a chair beside Ardal. "Explain."

"Last night we took care of such a problem." Ardal glanced over at Fiona. "The law protected a man who deserved to die."

Niail nodded. "So we do what others on this planet won't."

"Yes."

Silence filled the room. Ardal knew that he was right, but his men needed to believe it also. He could have blindly demanded they obey, but he wanted them to be part of the decision. This was the one truth that he had learned last night. It was wrong for others to dictate and control your life. If he were to continue to command his men, they must agree to it.

The Kaladin had used Hunters for their own purposes. They altered them, trained them, and demanded they do their killing. This was who he was and he would not deny his breed. What he found hard to forgive was that the Kaladin had denied them the simple gift of a mate.

They had done this out of fear and power.

No more. Ardal had broken with the past the moment he disobeyed the execution order. This was a new world with new rules. He would continue as he had begun.

"So we fight for those who cannot defend themselves." Firbin's voice held interest. "Do we charge for this service?"

"We must." Lorcan spoke now. "There is no other way to survive on this planet."

"You can charge those who can afford it." Fiona moved to Ardal's side. "You can trade services or favors with those who have no money."

He reached for her and pulled her onto his lap. She put her arm around his neck. He was complete. Fiona had given him that, not the Kaladin. He almost reeled under the surge of fierce protectiveness for Fiona.

Ardal looked at Lorcan. "How do we do this?"

"We advertise." Lorcan crossed his arms over his chest.

"What do we call ourselves?" Catal leaned forward on the table. "We need a new name if our mission is to change."

"Suggestions?" Ardal looked back at his men.

"We are Hunters, so people must understand that is what they are hiring." Niail glanced down at his coffee.

"You need something simple." Fiona leaned her head on his shoulder.

"Hunters for Hire." Catal grinned. "That's something you'd see in the want ads."

"Funny." Lorcan shook his head. "I hope you don't think that we'll advertise in the newspapers."

"The Internet is the best place." Catal tapped his finger on the table. "It will give us the anonymity that we need and the ability to access it from anywhere in the world. If we do it right, no one will find us."

"We will be safe?" Ardal was not going to risk anymore of his men's lives.

"Completely." Catal nodded. "Now we need a name for the website."

"aHunter4Hire.com." Fiona's voice rose in excitement. "Use the number 4 instead of the word for."

"That would work." Lorcan rubbed his chin. "You'd have to be careful that people won't misuse us, though."

Ardal frowned. "In what way?"

"Have us kill someone who wasn't guilty of any wrongs." Lorcan's voice was full of disdain. "Humans will often lie to get what they want."

"Then we will kill them." Niail spoke with quiet certainty.

Ardal locked eyes with Niail. He understood. There would be no room for mercy if a Hunter's honor was tarnished. The only recourse would be death. The code was very clear on this.

"Agreed." His decision was final. "We are Hunters. We will maintain our honor at all costs."

"That needs to be made clear on the website." Fiona's voice wavered. "You don't want any mistakes."

"The contract will be very precise and we will do surveillance before accepting a mission." Ardal looked at each of the Hunters around the table. "If we do this we must all agree."

Everyone gave their nod.

"I will contact the others and let them know the plan." Ardal pushed back his chair. "Now we need to find safety. Gur and Turlo will go west with Niail. The rest stay with me. We will set up the site and find a place to operate from."

Niail stood. "We leave in five minutes."

Everyone started to rise, but Lorcan's voice stopped them. "What about her?"

"Fiona stays with me." Ardal fought the urge to hit the man. "She is my mate. No Hunter can break that bond."

"Is that in the code that you're constantly quoting?" Lorcan's voice held suspicion.

"No." Ardal held Lorcan's gaze. "It will be though. We are no longer on Cygnus and neither the Holman, nor the Kaladin, control us. We are free men without implants. I may be the first to find my pair bond and mate, but I will not be the last."

"We've been on this planet longer than you and we've never found a mate."

"We didn't think that it was possible." Catal cleared his throat. "If we'd found our pair bond, would we have believed it?"

Lorcan looked at him for a few seconds before shaking his head. "No."

"This is a new world and a new beginning for us." Ardal let his words be understood before continuing. "We are no longer just Hunters. We are able to be men."

"You think this is possible for all of us?" Firbin's voice sounded hopeful.

"I know that it is." Ardal clenched his hand on the table. "The Kaladin denied us much when they took away our ability to find mates. I understand how important this gift is. I will not risk any of my brothers' chances of losing their pair bond."

"So a Hunter's mate must be protected?" Lorcan's voice held doubt.

"It is fitting." Niail spoke with quiet authority. "It is the honorable thing to do."

"Then it is so." Ardal pushed back his chair and stood with his arm around Fiona. "We begin a new life here. We will use our skills and talents to better our brotherhood. By Cygnus and Warrior we will thrive on this planet."

"Hunters true and right," Niail said before leaving the house. Turlo and Gur followed him.

The others began to gather equipment. They would take what was necessary for their new life. New identities and a new safe house were needed.

"Your life as the mate of a Hunter will not be easy." Ardal gathered her close.

Fiona leaned up and kissed his chin. "I enjoy adventure and new places."

"I promise that it will not always be so." Ardal brushed a strand of her hair from her face. "One day it will be safe for us to settle, but not now."

"I've been on the run for over a year. I know the score."

"I would wish a different life for you."

"I'll be happy so long as you're by my side." Fiona's eye sparkled with mischief. "Besides, who's going to protect you in this strange new land?"

Ardal squeezed her close and then set her free. "We need to leave."

"I'm ready." Fiona twirled in a circle. "I travel light. The clothes that I came in are all I have. You're the one with the heavy equipment."

Ardal grinned. He could never have predicted where his decision to disobey the execution order would lead him. Putting honor and duty to his men first, had led him to his mate. The path ahead was unsure and he would have to make choices, but there was doubt and question in all decisions.

From the Sacred Code he knew that great risks could bring much honor and reward.

Fiona was his reward. She gave him joy, purpose, and honor.

Author's Note

In November 1953, an American F-89 was scrambled from Kinross Airbase, north of Sault Ste. Marie, MI. to intercept an intruder that had shown up on radar. The fighter flew over Lake Superior for about thirty minutes before it was seen on radar to merge with the unknown aircraft, over Canadian airspace. After that, the F-89 signal was lost, but the intruder continued on its course for a while until its signal was also lost.

Algoma Central Railroad crews 100 miles north of Sault Ste. Marie, Ontario, heard a crash on the same night that the F-89 disappeared. There was also a report of a low flying aircraft before the crash.

In October of 1968 wreckage from an aircraft was found by two prospectors about 70 miles north of Sault Ste. Marie, Ontario. At the time this wreckage was thought to belong to the missing F-89, but the United States Airforce denied it.

In the 1950's, Wawa was an isolated area. The Algoma Central Railway was the only means of getting in and out of the community. Highway 17, also known as the Trans-Canada Highway, had not yet been completed. The search for the missing fighter was done from the air, but no wreckage was ever found.

There are many unanswered questions about this incident, beginning with why the fighter was scrambled in the first place?

The intruder was intercepted in Canadian airspace, so the concern over the unidentified aircraft had to be serious to take this action.

The official story was that the intruder was a C-47 aircraft that was flying 30 miles below its flight plan. The pilot of this aircraft denies that he was off course and his instruments were in good working order. Furthermore, he was contacted that night to see if he saw anything in the sky and reported that there was nothing within his sight. This means that the airbase in Kinross knew of his location and that he was flying in the area. He would not have been the unidentified intruder. This raises numerous questions:

Where is the wreckage of the F-89?

What happened to the intruder?

What crashed in the Limer area that night?

Were there any survivors?

Do Hunters walk among us?

For further information about this particular incident there is a more detailed account at:

http://www.ufobc.ca/kinross/index.htm

About the Author

Cynthia Clement began writing stories in her teens, but it wasn't until her forties that she became serious about writing. She lives in Canada with her husband of thirty years, her teenaged son, and two dachshunds. She has an eclectic range of interests including paranormal phenomena, ghost hunting, quilting, reading, gardening, and great conversation.

Her first book, The Seduction of Sarah, was a finalist in the HOLT Medallion Best First Book Category. Her novels, whether historical, paranormal, or science fiction, all focus on love, honor, and intrigue. To find out more information about her writing and books please visit her website: www.cynthiaclement.com

Look for more **aHunter4Hire** books.

Coming Soon

aHunter4Saken

www.ingramcontent.com/pod-product-compliance
Lightning Source LLC
Chambersburg PA
CBHW022201050726
47590CB00002B/606